THE TERRIBLE CHANGES

Published by Influx Press
Mainyard Studios
58B Alexandra Road
Enfield, EN3 7EH
www.influxpress.com / @InfluxPress
All rights reserved.
© Joel Lane, 2009, 2025

Copyright of the text rests with the author.
The right of Joel Lane to be identified as the author of this work has been asserted in accordance with section 77 of the Copyright, Designs and Patents Act 1988.

This book is in copyright. Subject to statutory exception and to provisions of relevant collective licensing agreements, no reproduction of any part may take place without the written permission of Influx Press.

This edition 2025.
Printed and bound in the UK by CPI.
First published in in 2009 by Ex Occidente Press
Paperback ISBN: 9781914391118
Ebook ISBN: 9781914391125
Cover design: Vince Haig
Interior design: Vince Haig

This book is sold subject to the condition that it shall not, by way of trade or otherwise, be lent, re-sold, hired out, or otherwise circulated without the publisher's prior consent in any form of binding or cover other than that in which it is published and without a similar condition including this condition being imposed on the subsequent purchaser.

JOEL LANE
THE TERRIBLE CHANGES

Influx Press
London

CONTENTS

Foreword	1
After the Flood	7
Power Cut	23
Empty Mouths	33
The Last Cry	53
Every Form of Refuge	63
The Hard Copy	81
Face Down	91
Tell the Difference	97
Blue Train	111
The City of Love	121
All Beauty Sleeps	129
The Brand	141
Alouette	151
The Sleepers	161
Acknowledgements	169

For Steve Green
And in memory of Ann Green –
these my dreams are yours

FOREWORD

NO LANGUAGE BUT A CRY

The contents of this book were chosen from my previously uncollected short stories in the weird fiction genre. In the process, it ended up as a retrospective of a quarter-century of writing – but also a collection with its own particular territory and purpose.

My main criterion was that each story needed to have an internal narrative, not just a plot. It had to communicate something. A number of stories written for professional anthologies ended up meaning less to me than stories simply written because their themes wouldn't leave me alone. I quickly found that the past stories of mine that I felt were worth reprinting were not the most horror-orientated ones, but the ones whose narratives *meant something* to me.

As a result, this collection tends towards the more low-key and private side of my writing. These are stories that really needed their own collection – and having chosen them, I felt that they belonged together. They are not presented in chronological order, though you can see the date of each story on the acknowledgements page. I've slightly revised a few of the earlier ones, but not really updated them in terms of whatever progress my approach to narrative has made.

A number of these stories appeared in classic magazines of the British weird fiction small press, such as *Dark Dreams*, *Exuberance*, *Skeleton Crew*, and *Dementia 13*. In those days, stories were retyped by the editor from typescripts, set by pasting strips of paper onto hardboard and illustrated with original line drawings – a far slower process than the integrated text-and-graphics package of desktop publishing, but one that gave each publication its own distinctive character.

When I started writing supernatural horror stories, it was under the influence of what I thought of as 'visionary' weird fiction: an approach I associated with such diverse writers as Arthur Machen, Walter de la Mare, Fritz Leiber, Robert Aickman, Harlan Ellison, Ramsey Campbell, and M. John Harrison. (And yes, I read stories by all of these writers in my teens. I was a deeply obsessive kid.) For all of these writers, the supernatural wasn't just frightening: it was meaningful. It carried a symbolic weight, like dreams or hallucinations. The 'unknown' was what we most feared to know.

Such early stories of mine as 'The Brand' and 'Tell the Difference' were trying, however clumsily, to dramatise the idea of an 'inner voice' that told people things they needed to know, but could not work out at a conscious level. As human relationships began to appear in my stories, the problems of intimacy became part of the supernatural content. And when political issues – money, power, war, corruption – became the focus, the supernatural content echoed the painful mixture of truth and distortion that characterises political discourse.

That's quite an agenda. In twenty-five years, I've hardly made a start.

By the early 1990s, I was beginning to gain a clearer sense of what I wanted to say in weird fiction. But the genre itself was starting to fragment. On the one side, many authors and fans seemed to be primarily interested in 'how far' they could go in terms of representing physical horror. That never greatly appealed to me. I'm quite squeamish, and whatever sexual taboos the genre imagined itself to be breaking had already been satisfyingly trashed by mainstream writers – Jean Genet, in particular, being a major influence on my writing.

On the other side, a new 'traditionalism' was forming that seemed to define itself largely through negative criteria. No violence! No sex! No 'bad' language! It didn't seem to matter to the devotees of this strand of supernatural fiction that the likes of Poe, Bierce and Machen had been fiercely unconventional and intensely sexual. I don't believe that sex and violence are equivalent in literary terms – to speak crudely (as one surely has a right to), sex is creative and violence is destructive. They are not part of the same agenda. As Ramsey Campbell has observed, much horror fiction makes violence a substitute for sex or even a punishment for it. Making weird fiction harmless and polite didn't seem to me a particularly creative approach.

JOEL LANE

Fortunately, I was able to tap into a rich new seam of what became known as 'slipstream' or 'miserablist' weird fiction, associated in particular with the great British independent press magazine *The Third Alternative*. While I didn't like the label 'slipstream' – to me, the best weird fiction had always been literary in both content and style – I loved what that approach meant for supernatural horror. It meant more of what I had always valued within the genre, and less of what I saw as one-dimensional and predictable.

By the new century, the intrinsic creative logic of the weird fiction genre had reasserted itself right across the board. Writers of overt horror had become more thoughtful. Writers of 'traditional' ghost stories had become more ambitious. Writers of 'slipstream' had woken up to the fact that that they had been writing either science fiction or supernatural horror all along.

I stopped caring about where I belonged and started to focus with some intensity on what I really wanted to say. I could see things coming apart, both within my life and in the world at large. The 'inner voice' was one I badly needed to hear. But, as Tennyson reminds us, it has *no language but a cry*.

Here are twelve previously uncollected stories, plus two brief new pieces. All were chosen primarily for what they try to say about the 'unknown' in our lives. Which, let's face it, is most of what we are and what goes on around us. Ghosts and other supernatural entities are metaphors not just for what we hide inside ourselves, but what we do not or will not understand in the world – including the very real threats of disease, madness and death, which we cannot tame or sanitise, but which may become a little less terrifying if we can see them more clearly.

That, in the end, is the most powerful agenda of the weird fiction genre: to help us confront the darkness. These stories, whatever their limitations, are part of my own struggle towards that goal. If there's nothing more to them than a cry, that's a start.

Joel Lane

AFTER THE FLOOD

Ironically for a town that had built its reputation on water, Leamington Spa had no provision for the flooding that took place on Good Friday 1997. Torrential rain caused the picturesque river that crossed the lower end of the town to overflow its banks, drowning several square miles of roads and surrounding fields. Commuters driving home for the bank holiday abandoned their cars in three feet of water. Houses, shops and restaurants were flooded out; cellars brimmed like teacups; bookcases exploded with the swollen volume of soaked paper. The battles over liability for the damage raged on for years.

Matthew had spent that weekend at his parents' house in Cardiff. By the time he came back, the flood had drained away. Most of the shops around the train station were closed, shutters and blinds hiding the damage. His bedsit was nearer the north end of town, higher up. The house clearly hadn't been affected. The newsagent at the end of the road told him: 'Lucky you were nowhere near the station. Trains didn't run all night. There's people drowned, cars ruined, no end of pets gone missing.' In the local paper, a Jehovah's Witness was quoted as saying: *It's a foretaste of things to come. This town must purge itself of the decadence that infects our streets.*

The house was quiet; most of the other tenants would be away for the whole Easter break. Matthew wanted to spend some time with Karen before the exam term got under way. She was his first proper girlfriend, and the passion they'd shared in the last couple of months had made it hard for him to focus on work. Karen wasn't a student: she worked in a little bookshop off the Parade. They'd met at Warwick University cinema, after a screening of *Blade Runner*. She'd changed everything for him: Leamington, his studies, being alive. Everything glittered with fragile sunlight.

Karen lived with two friends in a flat in Russell Street, not far from the station. He'd better call and check she was okay. The telephone rang four times; then he heard Karen's voice asking him to leave a message. He was about to speak when Sally broke in: 'Hello? Who's that?'

'Matthew. Hi. How are you?'

'Okay. Is Karen with you?'

'No.' He could still hear her voice in his head, wanted to answer it. 'I've been away since Friday.'

'So's Karen. We don't know where. Thought she might be with you. Her mum rang from Telford, so she's not there.' Sally breathed in anxiously. 'Shit... I hope nothing's happened to her. You know, the flood.'

'Jesus.' Matthew felt like he was drowning. 'Surely... surely by now... I mean...' She'd have been found, he wanted to say. Didn't want to say.

'You're right. Don't worry. When she comes in, I'll ask her to phone you straight away. If she's not here tomorrow, I'll go to the police. She'll be here, though. I just know it.'

But she wasn't. There were no leads to follow. No body was found. Sally talked to the police, who sent a DC to talk to Matthew. The young officer's questions were polite, but very detailed; Matthew knew he was under suspicion. It was hard to talk about Karen. They'd got very close quite quickly. He'd never expected to have to make factual statements to a stranger about sleeping with Karen; it felt cold and alien, a code for loss.

At the end of the interview, the DC said: 'We'll keep you informed. Let us know if you remember anything that might be helpful.' April slipped into May, and the police didn't get back to him.

As the weather grew warmer, the damage to the south side of town was gradually repaired. Shops and restaurants closed for refurbishment; cellar contents were piled in skips; the smell of rotting wood and plaster hung in the air like the ghost of last night's takeaway. Matthew was supposed to be preparing for his exams. But when the library closed, he'd drop off his books at home and then wander downtown towards the river. Maybe he'd pick up some clue about what had happened to Karen. But more, it was a way of keeping her alive.

One Friday evening, instead of having dinner, he drank four pints of Guinness at one of the pretentious new bars on the Parade. It was full of shouting Yuppies from local offices, grins like pale sharks. The bar was full of polished pseudo-rural artefacts: carvings, horseshoes, framed photos of show-jumping. The toilets were scented with pine. Staggering a little, Matthew walked down the Parade towards the River Leam where it came through Jephson Gardens. He'd expected the fresh air to clear his head; but it wasn't fresh. It seemed heavy, polluted by the traffic that clogged the town like cholesterol in blood vessels.

On the bridge, he gazed down at the waterfall. The setting sun and the tainted air made it look slightly yellow. He remembered standing here with Karen, around the same time in the evening. Her arm linked through his. How she'd said: 'I love rivers. They make me feel connected to the sea. It's a part of us, the sea. It's inside us.' They'd kissed then, and walked down past the station into the industrial part of town.

The canal ran parallel to the river, a shadow of it, like a sepia photograph. In between was a fault line of ruined or condemned buildings. That evening, they hadn't waited to get home. They'd found a bricked-up alley by the viaduct, out of sight of the road. The wall was tattooed with images and words. He remembered how she'd giggled when he'd stood on tiptoe to enter her: 'You're the wrong height.' And the way she'd bit his shoulder through the cloth in the last feverish moments, drawing blood.

Remembering, he was painfully aroused. Which only made him feel more wretched. He walked stiff-legged down to the end of the Parade, and along the viaduct. There were huts in the arches, pigeons nesting on corrugated-iron roofs. Blue plastic sacks were fixed across the gaps. Here was the alley, paved with broken glass and used condoms.

AFTER THE FLOOD

Graffiti covered the wall: PIGS SUCK, KERRY SMELLS OF EVERYTHING, COLIN IS FIT BUT HE TREATS GIRLS LIKE SHIT, GOTHS LIVE FOREVER. To one side, a wire fence was overgrown with some white flower he couldn't name. It smelt bad here.

Further south of the river, away from the grand architecture and the gift shops, most of the buildings were post-war: tenement houses and blocks of flats, workshops and little factories. A lot of students lived here. Karen had told him that this was supposedly the bad part of town, where it wasn't safe to be. It reminded him of the inner-city district where he'd grown up and gone to school. The 'spa town' part of Leamington – or, to give it its full Empire-building name, Royal Leamington Spa – left him cold. It made so much of its literary heritage; but the local branch of W.H. Smith's didn't stock a single literary journal. The town's sense of civic identity was embodied by the dark statue of Queen Victoria opposite the Municipal Baths, and the omnipresent signs banning drinking out of doors. The local paper had recently announced, with some pride, that a gay club had been denied a licence. The town's centre had a faintly decaying air of fifties pomposity that made him feel violent.

Out here, without a guidebook or tea-shop in sight, he was overwhelmed by thoughts of Karen. Her short reddish hair, pale blue eyes, freckles, conspiratorial smile. Her face on the pillow, asleep. Her frankness in bed: 'You can do anything you like, but don't make me pregnant. It's not up to me to take precautions, it's up to you.' The fact that most of what he remembered about her was sexual depressed him. He began to walk back towards the station, thinking about the first night they'd spent together. They'd been to see a film, and she'd come back to his room for coffee. Suddenly they'd started kissing. Then she'd drawn back and asked him something about the film. Without thinking, he'd said: 'Let's discuss it later.' She'd raised her eyebrows. 'You mean in the morning?' He'd wondered if he'd gone too far, and said awkwardly: 'You're reading my mind.' Then she'd smiled, put her mouth to his ear and whispered: 'No, just looking at the pictures.'

The weekend before his exams in June, Matthew decided to allow himself a Saturday night out. One of the tackier North Leamington bars was having a student night, with reduced prices and lots of gloomy 1980s music. He didn't intend to find someone, just to get drunk with his friends. But he was so hyper from studying and loneliness that he drank a lot without feeling the effects, and ended up drifting back and forth through the long venue on his own. The music made his grief sustainable, made it part of a world where everyone wore black. It mattered less that he and Karen wouldn't live together, have children, share a sunlit life.

There was a little bunch of Goths at the end of the bar, probably discussing whether it was worth the effort of forming a band. One of them glanced at him and smiled. She was short, stocky, with black hair and eyeliner – nothing like Karen. But in her brief smile, there was something that made Karen leap out of her face. He couldn't look away. She joined him at the bar. 'Are you having a bad night?'

'It's a long story. I'm okay.' He had to see that smile again. 'Are you in a band?'

'What, them?' Her teeth were smaller than Karen's; yet, somehow, the same smile. 'Yes, but we haven't put anything out yet. We're still absorbing influences.'

'What do you play?'

'The bass. Sometimes I sing. We swap roles quite a bit. We all live in the same house, so it's easy to work together.'

'Are you at the uni?'

'I work in the library.' He supposed she was a little older than him, but not much. 'You probably won't have seen me there. I'm an archivist. I've got my own office.' A graduate, then.

The barmaid was moving towards Matthew. 'Do you want a drink?' he said.

'Bacardi. Thanks.' They moved away from the bar. They talked about the university, his course, the bands that had played there recently. Her name was Terri. He couldn't place her accent; there was a trace of West Country in it – a diet lilt, so to speak – underneath the flattened Midland vowels. She seemed in no hurry to rejoin her housemates. They sat down together in the twilight of the lower bar, where it was quieter. Suddenly he was telling her about Karen. Her hand on his arm. Her face blurred by the tears in his eyes, changing.

'It must be dreadful,' she said. 'To lose someone and not even know where they are. But if you remember her, she hasn't completely gone.' Very gently, her fingers stroked a tear from his cheek. They looked at each other for a few seconds. Then they began to kiss.

Her mouth tasted of Bacardi. Like her smile, her kiss held faint echoes of Karen. He supposed that was how it always worked with new girlfriends. The same, but different. It didn't matter that Terri was a stranger, or that doing this made him think of someone else. She probably felt the same way. Why else was she giving herself like this? He felt her tremble in his arms. 'Are you all right?' he said. Her eyes were shut.

When the lights came up, she asked him: 'Do you want to come back with us?' They walked together through the backstreets of shuttered shops and glowing restaurants; across the park, where the pale bandstand stood like an empty cage; and down Brunswick Street, over the dark ribbon of the canal. Terri's housemates, two boys and a girl, walked with them – quiet, protective, almost like a family. Maybe he should get into this Goth thing. Terri gripped his hand. It was unusually quiet for this part of town: no dogs barking, hardly any traffic.

The house was one he'd walked past without really noticing. It had an overgrown front garden with poppies and hollyhocks. There was a small wooden gargoyle above the black front door. The windows were leaded. Inside, it seemed oddly formal: a hallway with a tiled floor, a bare staircase, blank walls. There was a peculiar smell of rotting wood and stagnant water, overlaid with chlorine like swimming baths. 'Sorry about the smell,' Terri said. 'The cellar was flooded. We're leaving it open to help it dry.' She put an arm around Matthew's shoulders. 'Let's go upstairs.'

Her room was almost as sparse as the hallway, though it had a double mattress under a duvet and a few Cure posters on the off-white walls. As he sat down, Matthew realised how drunk he was. The cracks in the ceiling were blurred. Terri bent down to kiss him. 'Would you like some vodka?' she asked. 'Russian.'

'I don't want to get too drunk,' Matthew said.

Terri looked steadily at him. 'Don't worry. We can make love in the morning.'

Matthew felt himself blushing. 'You can read my mind.'

Terri smiled. 'No, I'm just looking at the pictures.' Matthew felt a momentary chill. She took a bottle with a Cyrillic label from a small cupboard and filled two fluted glasses. It must be a line from some film they'd both seen. He kicked his shoes off.

The vodka tasted peppery and was exceptionally strong. It stung his lips. Gradually, he forgot the smell of the basement. They undressed each other in between sips of vodka. The tiny bedside lamp gave Terri a giant shadow, a face like paper over darkness. The room was cold; they slipped under the duvet, and Matthew fell asleep at once.

Towards dawn, he drifted in and out of sleep. There was a dripping tap somewhere, floorboards creaking, muffled voices. His limbs felt too heavy to move. He could hear Terri's steady breathing, but couldn't feel the warmth of her body. In his dream, he was walking down the house's uncarpeted staircase. It was twisted into a spiral, and it seemed to go on for ever. People were climbing past him, but he couldn't make out their faces. They seemed no more than shadows.

When he awoke, it was twilight. His muscles were tense, a reaction to the vodka. He was breathing fast. Terri slipped an arm across his chest and murmured: 'Relax, darling. It's all right. You're with me.' He lifted her onto him, and they kissed slowly. Her hand moved down his chest to his crotch.

'Wait,' he whispered, reaching for the packet of condoms he'd left beside the bed.

'Leave them,' Terri said. She caught his hand, guided it back under the duvet, pressed it to her taut belly. 'I want everything. Every trace of you. I can't have children.' He held her tightly; she was trembling again.

As the morning brightened outside, they made love furiously. Matthew was crying when they finished. A thousand sounds, movements and sensations reminded him of Karen. Was it his imagination, or was it always like this? The second time, it was easier to lose himself in the experience and forget what it meant. As he washed in the austere bathroom, he felt a sense of uneasy contentment. As if his loneliness hadn't gone away, but had been subdued by some kind of local anaesthetic. Sunlight melted through the net curtains, making indefinable shapes.

Over breakfast, they talked about work. 'I've got half a dozen books about narrative theory to look through for tomorrow's paper,' Matthew said. 'You never get time to actually read primary sources. Might as well be studying organic chemistry.'

Terri shrugged. 'What are you carrying books around for? This isn't the nineteenth century. You can get all that stuff off the Web.'

'I can't stand reading off a screen,' Matthew said. 'You lose any sense of context. A printed book is more meaningful. The way it looks tells you things. Besides, the Internet's making the use of sources totally confusing. At least before, to rip off somebody's ideas, you had to write them out. Now you just cut and paste, nobody's got any idea who's written what.'

'But what does it matter? It makes no difference whose words they are, if they're the right ones.'

They argued half-heartedly for a few minutes. In the kitchen, the alkaline smell from the cellar was hard to ignore. Matthew wished he'd got more sleep. 'I'd better get back,' he said. Their hands linked across the table. The shadows under Terri's eyes reminded him of her make-up the night before. They agreed to meet on Friday, after Matthew's last paper. In the dim hallway, they kissed goodbye with a passion he found almost frightening. She waved as he shut the garden gate and walked off in the burning, unreal sunlight.

All through the week, the staircase dream kept coming back. He never reached the foot of the stairs: they twisted down forever, past an unlit landing just a few steps away. Thoughts of Terri distracted him from work, especially in the library. His exams didn't go very well. And behind it all he still felt the loss of Karen, like a silence that nothing could fill.

An hour after completing his last exam paper, Matthew was standing on the bridge at the bottom of Jephson Gardens. He felt exhausted, relieved and nervous at the same time. Nervous because he'd not seen Terri since the morning in her room. Would she want to cool it? After all, she'd had a week to find someone better-looking, more experienced, taller. But here she was, still dressed in black, waving as she came towards him through the gardens' quilt of fertile colours. She embraced him. Their faces leaned together, hesitated, then kissed hard. The waterfall sang in his ears.

They walked along the riverbank, holding hands. Terri seemed less nervous than before; the sunlight had brought out a quiet energy in her face, a sense of self. Leaves cast faint, tattered shadows on the water. Up close, the yellow tinge of pollution was clear. He shivered. 'Are you all right?' she said.

'Yes. It's just... I can't seem to get away from water. Rivers, floods, canals.'

Terri gripped his arm. 'We're still in the sea,' she said. 'Wherever we are. Like crabs in pools. Just waiting for the tide.' He turned and looked into her eyes. They were dark, murky, but with a skin of light where he could see trees reflected.

They went for a drink at the Station Inn, which was just beginning to fill up with office and shop workers making a start to the weekend. The buzz of conversation mingled with the bleeping of mobile phones and cyberpets. Terri said her band, Forbidden Janet, were playing at the Haunch of Venison on Thursday night. Matthew said he'd be there. They both knew he only had nine days left before he went back to Cardiff for the summer. Under the table, their feet carried out their own slow, nervous conversation.

As they left the pub, Matthew suddenly knew what was going to happen. He didn't seem able to make decisions any more. They walked slowly to the crossroads at the foot of the Parade, and on to the canal and the traffic-blackened viaduct. The familiar smell of stagnant water. The broken glass in the alley. A scrap of torn plastic raised its head and flapped away. Terri backed against the wall, held him against her. As he lifted her in his arms, she giggled. 'You're the wrong height.' They made love quickly, without foreplay. Matthew was shaking so much that he hardly needed to move. Terri bit his shoulder when she came. Her teeth were sharper than Karen's.

They went back to Terri's house, where they shared a bath and made love again, splashing in the antique claw-footed tub while steam drew ghostly figures in the mirror. Then Terri cooked them some pasta with mushrooms and shredded chicken. She seemed to sample food, eating a little bit of everything without getting through much; but she drank a lot of wine. They both did. At the back of his mind, Matthew thought he should ask Terri what she really knew about Karen. But he couldn't find the right words. Instead, they talked about records. Terri's favourite Cure album was *Disintegration*; Matthew's was *Faith*. They both thought Nirvana's *In Utero* was a better album than *Nevermind*.

Around midnight, they climbed the naked stairs to Terri's room, where they drank some more Russian vodka and listened to a tape of Forbidden Janet. It was strong on rhythm, but weak on dynamics. Like most Goth bands. Terri said the rest of the band were off to see the bright lights of Kenilworth. They'd be back later. Matthew knew only the alcohol was keeping him awake. Fibres of smoke from Terri's cigarettes made the air seem tangible. He could still make out the faint odour of bleach and decay from the basement. When the music faded, they lay together on the mattress, naked, not moving.

The air was damp and cool. He could hear something from below, within the house: a whispering like the sea, a gradual sifting of layers. The smell of rot was stronger now. It must be rising through the walls. He could feel sunlight on his back and the side of his face. His mouth was so dry that his breath seemed to stick to it. He sat up and rubbed his eyes.

Terri was sleeping beside him, stretched out on the duvet. Her face was shifting, changing its expression. She didn't look like Terri. The mouth twisted, and something moved under the skin of her cheek. One eyelid swelled like a blister, then fell inward. He didn't know what he was seeing. It was the vodka, he realised, tasting his own sweat in his mouth. He reached out to touch her arm. It was cool: no sign of fever. Then the arm lifted towards him, coiling. It seemed to have no bones. It was hardly an arm at all.

He backed off, pressing his hand to his mouth. A thread of darkness flickered behind his eyes. With shaking hands, he pulled on his jeans and walked as quietly as possible out of Terri's room and down the stairs. Light hung in the dusty air by each window, like patches of cloth. The smell of decay was stronger in the hall, mixed with something else: flesh and brine, like a crowded swimming pool. He could hear water swirling round and round, very slowly. The sound was coming from the basement.

He pushed at the door under the stairs. Paint flaked away on his fingers; the wood felt soft, yielding. It wasn't locked. A wave of decay hit him. Somehow, it didn't seem like a smell of death. He walked down five cold steps. There was a faint light in the basement, but he couldn't see any window. No light bulb either. Just four walls, and the bluish tint of whatever was covering the floor.

It was like a swamp of some kind: mould and peat and stagnant water, with crusts and ripples on its uneven surface. It smelt brackish, like seawater left out in the sun. Like rock pools. And it was moving. He could make out shapes just under the surface: hands, shoulders, the curve of a spine. And then he could see the faces. A dozen of them, more, their eyes filled with a faint violet glow. And among them, Karen. She saw him and smiled.

Suddenly he understood what the staircase dream meant. And what Terri had meant about working in the library. The library was here. His hands began to unfasten his jeans. There was no choice to be made. It had already happened. Naked, he stepped forward into the murky pool. It lapped around his feet, gripping them. The steps went on under the surface. He could feel the pool absorbing him, reading his flesh like a phrasebook. It was deep enough to drown in. Its texture was dense, blood-warm, intimate. It was memory.

In the last moment, her face slipped over his.

POWER CUT

The procession started in Chamberlain Square and moved along New Street, thinning out as the roadway narrowed. There were several hundred people, wearing overcoats against the iron wind; it was early December. Each of the marchers carried a lit candle in a glass jar or paper shield. Every so often, one of them would stop to relight a flame that had blown out. Above their heads, premature Christmas lights hung from wires strung across the roadway.

At this time in the evening, there wouldn't be much traffic for the procession to interrupt. As usual Lake felt he'd been singled out. He waited in a side road, watching the passing figures from his car. Candlelight gave their hands and parts of their faces a peculiar glow. Lake wished he could drive through them. Who were they trying to impress? There was nobody around to pay attention. Minutes passed, and the number of marchers began to unnerve him.

His flat had been empty since the previous weekend. It was colder than he expected. There were only a few letters for him; but then, most of his correspondence went through his office in London. Not many people knew his private address. Lake put a takeaway meal into the oven to warm up, and lit the gas fire in the living room. He was just in time for the local news round-up on Central TV. Sure enough, there was a mention of the candlelit procession; and similar events in other cities.

The week before, they'd quoted Lake as saying that to spend public money on a local hospice for AIDS victims would be to betray the local community.

The hold that the welfare state lobby seemed to have over the media didn't impress Lake at all. Why should ordinary people have to shoulder the responsibility for AIDS? Besides, there were deeper issues at stake. To modernise the health service was an essential step towards the new society. The Midlands had to be dragged out of the mire of 1950s welfare state apathy, and brought to life the same way as was happening in the South. So many people just didn't seem capable of understanding. Even his own party didn't have the clarity of purpose it had had a few years back. Things weren't making sense; the leadership had crumbled. But Lake refused to panic. He felt strangely calm, sitting in the silent flat, and still cold in spite of the gas fire; it was as though the blue flames were only for display.

He tried calling Alan, but heard only a disembodied voice telling him to leave his name and number. Lake felt suddenly at a loss for words. Just before the machine cut out, he managed to speak. 'It's David. Ring me.' They hadn't seen each other in weeks, but Lake knew he could depend on Alan. The thought was a flicker of symbolic warmth.

The next morning, he wondered if something had been wrong with the takeaway; perhaps he shouldn't have reheated it. But he didn't have the normal symptoms of food poisoning – gut pains, nausea, diarrhoea. It felt more as though something inside him were coated with frost. He rubbed the mist from the bedroom window, then breathed it back in place. The room was chilly, but well above zero. Outside, the day was unexpectedly bright.

After breakfast, which he couldn't taste, Lake phoned his doctor. The receptionist took a message, but wouldn't make him an appointment. 'Dr Wilson will contact you as soon as possible, I'm sure.' Well, he'd intended to have a quiet weekend; he needed a break from work. It would be Christmas soon, and there were people he had to get in touch with – friends and family. He'd been headbutting the brick walls in Westminster for too long; he was lonely. Realising that made him feel paralysed. What if nobody was there?

It was noon when he phoned Alan. This time there was an answer. 'Hello? Who's that?'

'Alan, it's me.' There was no response. 'It's David. How are you?'

'Oh, I'm fine. No problems.' There was a silence. Lake felt it stretch across twelve miles of telephone cable, like a thread leading him into a maze of blind tunnels. He took a deep breath; still silence.

'Alan. Are you there?'

'Yes. What can I do for you?' The voice was deliberately empty of anything recognisable. Why was Alan pretending to be a stranger?

'Can I see you?'

'Yes. If your X-ray telescopic vision is in working order. We're on opposite sides of the city, after all. Then there's the curvature of the Earth to consider. And you're probably facing in the wrong direction anyway.' More silence. 'Where were you when I needed you, David? Where would you be now if I still did? Where would I be if I still did? Tell me something.'

'What?... Go on, what is it?'

'Do you know what flowers grow in winter?' Lake wasn't sure he'd heard that correctly; but the next sound was the click of the receiver. He went on listening to the dead line for minutes, like a child pressing a shell to his ear to hear the sea.

Lunch tasted of less than breakfast. Midway through the afternoon, Lake switched on the TV and watched an hour of soap opera. The rage and torment of the characters stuttered in his mind. He blinked away tears and felt them trickle to the corners of his mouth, where he tasted their fresh salt. Feeling somewhat better, he phoned his doctor and got the receptionist again. 'Dr Wilson's not available. There's no space in his appointment schedule. I'm sorry.' Lake stared at the receiver as if it had bitten his ear. Well, he'd have to hire another doctor.

He didn't have to wait for help.

It was dark by four o'clock, and far colder than the morning had been. Lake typed out a series of letters to constituents on the solid Underwood typewriter he kept at home. His sense of perspective restored, he went out for a short walk. As far as the off-licence and back again. Harborne's streets were reassuringly empty. Rain shattered the windscreens of parked cars. Through a few uncurtained bay windows he saw glass flowers, bookcases, paintings hung on dark-panelled walls. Lake felt a shock of loss, and didn't understand why. He'd always fought his own battles. It didn't seem to matter that he had no friends. He'd been a grammar-school pupil; there was no old-boy public school network to support him. He believed in power and the respect that power earned. You could trust authority; you couldn't trust people.

The way back took him under a railway bridge that crossed the main road. A car came up the hill towards him; and in the same moment, a train flickered past overhead. Lake felt as though his heart had stopped. He stood quite still. To one side, the streetlamp lit up points of rain on the dark thorns of a shrub. He reached out and touched them. They pricked his hand, without breaking the skin. He drew his hand back and pressed it against the flat bottle in his coat pocket. What was wrong with him?

Lake ate alone, at home. This seemed to have been the most isolated and purposeless day of his life. Something had to change. He phoned Alan, but put down the receiver before it could ring at the other end. Alan had sounded disturbed; he was evidently having problems. It wasn't Lake's business to help. Things like that were beyond him. How was he going to make this weekend a success? By eight o'clock, the whisky was at least a technical fire in his stomach and mind. He'd have to hit town tonight. But he'd better not drive in this condition.

And which town? He didn't want to risk being recognised.

Secrecy, he thought, was not only necessary but correct.

The train to Wolverhampton took him through Dudley and Tipton, past empty and poorly-lit streets whose terraced houses were more than a century old. Security lights flooded the ground floors of the factories. Whenever the carriage window looked onto darkness, Lake saw his own face flicker across the view. He was shivering, like his reflection. A copy of the *Express & Star* was spread face down on the seat opposite; he picked it up and tried to read better news into its headlines. The sports pages at the back were easier to follow, because they meant nothing to him.

He caught a taxi from the station to the club, though he could have walked there in a few minutes. The centre of Wolverhampton was surprisingly quiet for a Saturday night. The sky was cloudy; mist made the upper air a canvas for the town's light. A car park jumped in perspective, becoming a cobbled yard. Everything bright seemed closer than it was; and warmer, too. Lake felt himself sobering up. He'd have to reverse that.

Two hours later, he was walking back along the same route.

His companion was a tall youth in a grey leather jacket and black jeans; his name was Gary. He lived in a rented room on the other side of town. It was too late to go back to Birmingham, and Lake wouldn't have wanted that anyway. This arrangement suited him; he understood business better than he understood people. Why was he doing this? It wasn't recklessness, he knew that. With Alan it might have been, if he hadn't tried to hedge his bets. Now it was more like giving himself up. The cold shifted inside him, touching him as he breathed. In the club, nobody had spoken to him or given him a second glance. He'd have to pay to get what he wanted. Which proved he'd been right all along.

POWER CUT

Gary's room was in a terraced house opposite a paper yard, where flaking white blocks were piled up as if to thaw them out. There was a long series of bell-buttons next to the front door. The unlit hall smelt of fresh cat urine. Moving quietly, Gary led his client up the uncarpeted staircase. Three flights, each with a time-switch to restore darkness. Lake imagined he could follow Gary by sensing his body heat, even at a distance.

Suddenly, he felt an absolute need for physical contact – a strange feeling that seemed to have no connection with what was going on. A wall opened into a small but high-ceilinged bedroom, decorated with faded newspaper cuttings and photographs. The floor was littered with envelopes, notebooks and old newspapers, the pages merged by damp. It was more like a press office than a bedroom. If Gary was going to bring people back here, he really should keep the place tidy. Was he a student? Gary sat down on the bed and lit a cigarette. Lake sat beside him, feeling too cold to unbutton his coat.

'Can you put the fire on?' Gary shrugged in reply, as if to say *What fire?* His cigarette brightened as he inhaled, which made the wall behind him seem darker. Lake stretched his arms, biting back a yawn. Why were there so many newspaper cuttings on the walls? He couldn't read any of the headlines.

Shadows were falling on every exposed surface, like dust. But there was no lampshade. Lake stared at the naked light bulb, hanging from a cord in the centre of the whitewashed ceiling.

Its light was slowly weakening. No, it was still as bright as before. But the darkness was pressing in around it. Lake shook his head and stood up. 'God, I'm pissed.' Gary watched him without making a comment. Something on the wall caught Lake's attention: a news item that looked familiar. He stood close to it. His own breath stung his lips.

The plaster of the wall was almost covered with cuttings from local and national newspapers. Every mention in print of anything that Lake had said or done – even where his name appeared in election results or candidate lists – was here. Several of the cuttings displayed his face, a blur of dots on yellowed paper. His appearance hadn't changed much in ten years. Lake turned round. 'What the fuck is this?' Gary was still lying on the bed, propped up on one elbow and almost smiling, like a picture in a magazine. He blew a smoke-ring.

Lake pulled at one of the sheets of newsprint. It was glued to the wall, but most of it came away. He tore down another cutting; then several at once. Underneath, the plaster was surprisingly clean and whole. He felt a streak of cold along the side of his hand, and saw the head of a rusty nail protruding from the wall. Blood immediately began to spread on the cuff of his right sleeve, like a flower petal or an oil flame. 'Oh, Jesus.' He turned back to the bed. 'I've cut my hand.' Gary looked and nodded, but didn't move. Lake sat down beside him. Blood splashed onto the pale blue duvet. It dulled at once, becoming a shadow. Lake tried to pull his sleeve up over the cut. 'Help me. I could get blood poisoning.' He stared at the boy. 'Help me. Please!' Quite calmly, Gary reached out, took Lake's hand and stubbed out his cigarette on it. There was no cruelty in the action. It was exactly as though the hand were an ashtray. Lake felt the cold stiffen inside him, blind and enclosed, like a fist. He couldn't open his mouth. Slowly, trying to balance himself, he stood up, then walked out into the unlit hall. A few seconds later, the bedroom door closed behind him.

Outside, the street was empty; Lake tried to remember the way back into town. He could see the distant lights of tower blocks around the station. It seemed to get colder the further he walked. The wind felt like having crystals of frost rubbed into your skin. He thrust his hands into his coat pockets, careless of the bloodstains. But when his right hand stuck to the coat lining, he had to pull it free. In the metallic light of the streetlamp, he saw white threads of snow glittering at the edges of the wound. His legs were shaking too much for him to walk.

Was there nobody to help him? Ahead of him, he could see people crossing the road, on their way down another street. He tried to catch up with them. As he neared the corner, he saw that each of them was carrying a light.

The street was lined with dark, unrecognisable office buildings; there were very few doorways. People were walking along the roadway and the pavements, with lit candles in their hands.

Lake couldn't see how many people there were; but white petals of wax were already scattered across the tarmac. He stepped forward.

'Help me.' Silent figures walked past him on both sides. They didn't seem to notice Lake, or even to notice each other. Lake stood directly in front of one of them, daring the marcher to walk through him. But the man stopped, looking at Lake with candles in his eyes. Others stopped too, until Lake was surrounded in the middle of the road. There were a dozen or more of them. The rest of the procession moved on. In the circle of lights, Lake could see that the marchers' faces were covered with wax.

A gap appeared in the circle. One of the candles had gone out. Lake felt the ache in his hand disappear, as though the wound had closed. Another gap. He couldn't feel the cold in his chest now. He touched his own face, and felt nothing.

Three more candles went out. The taste of the air had gone, and the smell of burning wax. Lake turned around; a ripple of dark shivered in the air. There were only four candles left. He cried out: *Help me, don't leave me. Please.* But he couldn't hear his own voice. He carried on begging silently, making gestures.

Drops of wax fell and froze around him like snow. The holder of the last candle was standing close by. If only Lake could reach his face to pull off the wax mask, he would have made contact. He was lifting a hand when the stranger bent his head to blow out the flame and with it, the streetlamps.

EMPTY MOUTHS

The off-licence was round the corner from Claire's flat. They sold draught sherry at a low price; you took in bottles and they filled them. There were two young prostitutes in the shop, dressed in leather jackets, boots and mini-skirts. A third was standing outside, watching the traffic. But the roads were almost empty. It was cold for November, and mist hung between the buildings. The streetlamps trailed showers of orange light. Walking home, with two bottles chiming together in a plastic carrier bag, Claire felt exposed by the lack of visibility.

The doorway had been clear ten minutes earlier. But now, there was a man crouching on the steps. Claire had to pass him, open the door and switch on the hall light before she could see who it was. As she did so, the stranger moved. It was the old man who lived on the second floor. His face was a jigsaw of blood; the right eye was closed. Against his pale skin and white hair, the blood was something unreal, like stage make-up. His good eye stared at Claire without recognition, and he tried to speak. He had a strong Scots accent; Claire couldn't make out the words. She shook him. 'Are you all right?' He stood up, leaning against the doorframe, and pushed past her into the hallway. At the foot of the stairs, he turned round and mouthed a word, without speaking. Then he began to climb the stairs.

Claire stood in the hallway, shivering. She didn't know if he'd passed out from alcohol or shock. His clothes stank of wine. Sometimes in the night, she'd heard him struggling to open the front door, then thumping into walls and furniture, and singing to himself. Perhaps she ought to call an ambulance; that wound could have damaged his eye. More than the blood, what had worried her about his face was the impression of a different face under it. But that was an effect of the mist outside, or the light reflecting off blood and spittle. The submerged face had seemed thin and scared. Like a child's image. There were splashes of blood in the thin carpet of the hallway, darkening as they merged with footmarks and dead leaves.

Back in the flat, Robert was watching a horror video. The only light in the room came from the flickering screen, alternately white and red. He was holding a can of lager; the remnants of a four-pack were perched on the arm of the couch. 'All right?' he said as Claire walked past with the carrier bag. 'You should watch this one. It's not bad.'

Claire stood behind him, looking at the screen. Robert's hair trailed down the back of the sofa behind his head. His refusal to get it cut was one of the things she liked about him. They were still close, though they no longer slept together;

neither of them had felt like moving out. In the dim light, it was difficult to make out his hair against the fabric of the couch. Somebody tried to scream and choked on blood. 'What's it about?' Claire said.

Robert half turned his head, smiling in profile. 'Not a lot. It's just a cynical view of horror clichés. The victims are more disgusting than the killers. They're all complete arseholes, basically.' His face twitched back to the screen as a shower of blood fell against the glass. It sounded dry, like sand. A man leaned forward and vomited an entire kidney; presumably his own, Claire thought. She didn't feel like telling Robert about the injured drunk. It must be the man in Flat 11, who received post under four different names (three of them conspicuously Scottish). She took the lager can from Robert's hand, drained it and gave it back to him. 'Cheers, lover,' he muttered without turning his head.

Her bedroom was cold. Claire lit the gas fire and sat on the unmade bed, feeling rather isolated. There was a coffee mug on the floor near her feet, with a cigarette stubbed out in it. It wasn't hers. Claire tried to remember his name. 'Bastard,' she said quietly, not knowing quite who she meant. A patch of damp in the far corner of the room was shading in the wallpaper's pattern. On the mantelpiece, a gilt-edged mirror accused her of getting older. 'Shit.'

Where was there to go to? Moseley Village was losing its appeal, somehow. All her friends seemed to be moving away; or else losing their energy, becoming static. From month to month their lives didn't change; there was hardly any need to keep in touch. Near midnight, the phone rang; it was Stella. She wanted to meet Claire for coffee the next afternoon.

JOEL LANE

Saturday was normally the only good day in the week. Claire got up early and went shopping in the Village, while it was still quiet. A cold flame of mist hung around the trees on the park's boundary. Claire thought she could smell burning, though no smoke was visible. She bought fresh bread, vegetables, steak, some red wine and a cheap woollen scarf. Outside the church on the main road, half a dozen or so drunks were sitting on wooden benches. More were sprawled in the entrance to Tesco's. Not all of them were vagrants; many, like the white-haired man in Claire's house, had lodgings in the district. But the street was somewhere to go, for company if nothing else. Then there were the lost-looking old people from the DSS hostel for ex-mental patients, who spent all day and half the night wandering in the streets. They must go round in circles, since they kept reappearing. Nobody paid them any attention.

Claire liked this district. It was where a lot of non-local people ended up, a shelter for outsiders. Birmingham was divided between the inner city and the suburbs; each was oppressive in a different way. But Moseley didn't fall into either category. Its tall grey-fronted houses, with bay windows and rusty fire escapes, harboured families of Victorian ghosts. The real tenants were different. Nearly all of the larger houses were tenements, their thin-walled flats and bedsits occupied by students, punks, artists and drug users. Moseley was full of the kind of improvised families or sub-communities that formed between people who shared the same house, studied at the same college, or were linked by their way of life. For all that, the usual oppositions cut through the district. The vagrants and prostitutes were a sign of the division. So was the fact – disturbing, but by no means mysterious – that there were three or four times as many off-licences here as pubs.

Stella lived in a cramped bedsit off the Alcester Road, on the edge of Balsall Heath. Claire called in the early afternoon. As usual, they embraced; Stella was quiet and rather tense. She made some filter coffee, and they exchanged anecdotes about work. Claire had once been a typesetter for the same company that Stella worked for. Stella hadn't had the confidence to leave. While Claire's bedroom always gave the impression of vacancy, Stella's was crowded. Art prints and record sleeves reduced the wallpaper to margins. Paperbacks were piled up along the skirting-board; damp had curled their front covers. Traces of candle wax gleamed on the mantelpiece. That was one of Stella's problems. She couldn't tidy away the past: it all had to be there, unchanged, from year to year.

But what was troubling her now was Martin. They'd been seeing each other on and off for the past two years. Recently, rather to Claire's alarm, they'd been talking about getting married. 'Most of the time he's all right. But he's been in some really weird moods lately. Especially when he's drunk. He just goes off on his own. He's like a different person, I can't talk to him. One night... Janet told me he ended up in her house. He must have slept with Neil.' *Not again*, Claire thought. Stella's eyes raked the walls with a ritual anger. 'He must have been really out of it, too. He's not like that any more... He said so.'

'Well, he would, wouldn't he?' Claire said.

'If he stopped drinking it would be different. I'm sure. Drunks don't have any... like, sexual identity. Do they? They're just bodies.'

'Unlike the rest of us.'

Stella looked wounded. 'Why are you so sharp?'

'Don't know. Something broke, I suppose.' Probably living with Robert had given Claire the habit of rapid-fire cynicism. She disliked herself a great deal sometimes. 'Stella, I think you're just... well, holding on to the wrong person.'

'But he keeps coming back to me. He needs me.'

'Yes,' Claire said. 'But have you asked yourself why?'

Stella shivered. 'Shit, it's cold in here.' She fumbled with matches, lighting the gas fire. 'How's Robert?'

'Same as ever. He's got his videos and his comics. He's happy. No problems.' Claire smiled. 'We're all right as friends. Sometimes you have to admit defeat.' She thought about the dozen or so men she'd brought home in the last few months. How many of them were just to score points off Robert? But each new affair helped her work out the past. Perhaps one day she'd find the man in whom she could bury all the others. And then he'd go, leaving no mark on her, and she'd be free. Her spine twitched suddenly, pulling her back into the room. 'Sorry. I was just... daydreaming.' It was dark outside.

Walking home in the sudden chill of late afternoon, Claire thought about Martin and Stella. Why had they stuck together for so long? The question she'd thrown at Stella had been unfair. But what made Martin stay with a woman he didn't love? And what made Stella keep trying with a man she knew was homosexual? It was an old pattern, repeating itself without ever making any sense, like an argument between two drunks in a pub.

Slow cars were pacing the streets from corner to corner; their headlights stared vacantly at the mist. At the foot of

Strensham Hill, a young girl was shivering in a mini-skirt and short leather jacket. Christ, she'd die of exposure if she didn't get picked up soon. Claire felt helpless with rage. She could see why they dressed like that, however cold it was on the street. Their obvious vulnerability made them more attractive to men haunted by their own powerlessness. Claire was past feeling threatened by the kerb-crawlers. Their cars made her think of supermarket trolleys. Just outside her house, another car stopped; another teenage girl got out and stood waiting by the kerb, her arms wrapped tensely across her blue T-shirt.

The hallway was unlit, but Claire glimpsed a whitish blur near the foot of the stairs. She couldn't make out what it was, or exactly where. When she pressed the time switch, two figures appeared. One was standing. He looked like a teenage boy, though his face was older. His mouth was a perfect circle of shock. Slowly, he pulled his hand away from the other figure's face; his fingers seemed abnormally long. The stairway creaked. Then there was only one person. He was still lying there, face up. It was the tenant who'd cut his face the night before. His left eye was a raw bruise; the right eye was staring open. Claire moved nearer, listening for his breath. Close up, she could see that his face and neck had been cut into many times. The wounds had all closed to white lines, sunk into the skin. She touched his mouth: the lips were cold. The skin stuck to her fingers and tore when she pulled away. Claire gripped the wooden stair post and held onto it until she was steady again.

Robert phoned the police, then poured Claire a drink and made her sit down near the fire. Slowly her mind cleared, and she couldn't be sure what she'd seen. By then, Robert and several other tenants had seen the dead man. He'd apparently suffered a heart attack, since he was unmarked except for a black eye. The police and the ambulance men were gone within half an hour. Claire wondered briefly who the child with the adult face could have been. Then she realised that shock could create false memories. The confusion made her start to cry silently. Robert put his arms around her and they stood in the chilly living room for minutes, holding onto each other without speaking.

That evening, they were both going out: Claire was meeting some friends in the Village, and Robert was going into town. 'Are you sure you'll be okay?' he said. 'I can stay in if you like.'

Claire shook her head. 'Don't worry. I don't want to stay here anyway, it's not healthy.' The pub would shake her out of herself. Besides, she thought to herself, if she and Robert stayed in tonight they'd probably end up sleeping together, which might make the situation worse. Robert walked with her up to the main road, then caught the bus.

The Village was full of people Claire knew, including Stella and Martin. It was only nine o'clock, but Martin was well gone. Stella was sitting alone, looking miserable. Claire spoke to her, but she didn't want to talk. Martin, his eyes bloodshot, struggled to down a pint while persuading one of his friends that Britain could never become a democracy until the Royal Family were executed in public. Claire snapped at him: 'Do-it-yourself socialism gives capitalism an excuse.' Martin laughed, then went quiet. For a moment, he didn't seem to know where he was.

Half an hour later, Claire was talking with a thin, quiet lad she'd never seen before. His name was Andrew. He

EMPTY MOUTHS

came from Stirchley, which Claire thought would be enough to make anyone mute. He bought her a drink; but as she took it from his hand, Claire saw Martin going out the door alone. She touched Andrew's arm. 'Wait here. I just have to speak to someone.'

Martin was on the corner of Woodbridge Road before she caught up with him. 'Where are you going?' He stared at her, then turned and walked on. The streetlamp made his face and breath glow a damp white.

On the canal bridge just beyond the police station, Martin stopped and leaned over the water. He appeared to be screaming, but Claire couldn't hear anything. Then he stood back and wiped his mouth. His hand was shaking; his teeth chattered. 'What's wrong?' Claire said. Martin stared again, not seeing her. He wrapped his arms over his chest and vomited slowly onto the pavement. Claire turned away and then couldn't turn back. She felt detached, like a sleepwalker; as though she could walk through fire and not feel it.

When she got back to the pub, Andrew was still there. He smiled at her. 'I knew you'd come back.'

'Of course. I was just worried about someone.' She tried to explain about Martin. 'I think there's something wrong with him. But if Stella can't help him, what can I do?' The pub was filling up now, mostly with young local people – punks, students, schoolkids nervously trying to score dope or cheap pills. Two girls in denim jackets were kissing discreetly under the staircase. Claire felt a moment of jealousy. She liked men, but hated their vacancy and selfishness in bed. The CD jukebox was playing a Joy Division track, painful in its clarity. The bass notes made the light tremble. 'Why do you come here?' she said to Andrew.

'Well, it's somewhere to go. All the Stirchley pubs are full of old men rotting away. Feel like a prisoner, the whole time.' Andrew's mouth twitched as he spoke. 'It's so lonely at home,' he said. 'A bedsit in a house full of people I don't know. Do you live round here?'

'Just down the road. Got a flat. Shared; my flatmate's a bloke. I quite like the place... Some of the other tenants are a bit weird. There was an old Scottish wino on the second floor who drank himself to death.' Andrew was reading her lips. A lot of people did that in pubs where the music was too loud. She leaned forward, speaking into his ear. 'Do you want to come back and see the flat?' Why was it always so easy?

They walked back along Chantry Road, an indirect route that was quieter and more attractive than the main road. Andrew blinked at the warning sign: 'What's that? A frog warning?'

Claire laughed. 'Yes. Warning to drivers. There's a pond on one side of the road, and in spring the frogs cross the road from people's back gardens and cellars; they all converge on this pool and fuck.'

'How do they know where to go?'

'Same as everyone else, I suppose. The word gets round. You know. *All-night party in the bit of wasteland near Cannon Hill, bring your own mucous membrane.* Some of them stop off at the chemist's for a pack of condoms on the way.' Andrew laughed quietly. Claire had seen the frogs on the road in March; the sight had unnerved her completely. As they walked along, she held onto his arm. The wind blew dead leaves through the chain-link fence and made them finger the tarmac like infant hands. The houses were all well-groomed, fronted with dry-stone walls and unusual trees. A few warning lights flashed on as Claire and Andrew passed, then went out. Andrew put his arm around Claire's waist; she touched his hand, which was cold. *My lover*, she thought, trying to give herself confidence.

Robert was already back when they arrived. To his credit, he said nothing except 'Hello'. Andrew declined the offer of coffee. Claire led him to her room, and put on a Pale Saints album to drown the sounds of cannibalism from Robert's video.

They waited for the room to warm up; the situation inhibited them both. Andrew paced around the bed, looking uneasy. He drew back the curtain from the window and stared at the building opposite. 'Look at that. Is that a prison?'

Claire looked past his shoulder. 'No. It's some kind of hostel.'

'Why has the upper room got bars on the window?' He wouldn't look away from it.

'I suppose, if it was a Victorian house, that room was the nursery. The bars were to keep children safe. Why? Does it matter?' Andrew shook his head and drew back. He sat on the narrow bed and looked slowly round the walls, taking everything in. Claire sat down beside him. His face was trembling. 'Is anything wrong?' Andrew looked at her. She hadn't realised until now how dark his eyes were. You'd think he'd spent his life crying. Slowly, he shook his head. Then he pulled her shoulders down to the bed and kissed her, closing his mouth over hers. He drew breath from her lungs. They undressed in the dark and climbed awkwardly in between the cold sheets.

Almost at once, Claire felt shut in by her memories. Every contact with the other's body gave life to some partial ghost. They lay side by side, exploring each other with hands and mouths. Andrew's chest was smooth, the flesh tight over the bones. His prick jutted out at an oblique angle; she kept knocking into it by mistake. Claire wondered how it felt to have this blunt knife attached to your lower body, neither a part of yourself nor a part of the outside world. She sucked him until his body grew tense; then she sat up and tried to make out his face in the darkness. An edge of white light passed between the curtains; the gas fire, on its lower setting, flickered blue and orange. She kept imagining a boy with long fingers and a huge mouth. He whispered something; she whispered back 'I'll do it,' and reached into the bedside cabinet for a packet of Durex Gold. The absurdity of the foil wrapping was itself a kind of protection.

They made love with an almost painful slowness, clinging together under the blanket. Claire had no sense of herself. There was one body in the room, or else many. She couldn't come, because the shape of her identity kept slipping and changing. The more closely she and Andrew locked together, the more difficult the rhythm became. For both of them, release seemed impossible. Eventually they drew apart and masturbated separately. Claire drifted into an uneasy sleep. She woke up several times in the night and saw Andrew lying awake, staring at the window. She could hear the sound of rain. Andrew's tension kept her at a distance. She realised she'd never wanted to get to know him. In the half-light just before dawn, Andrew got out of bed and began dressing. Claire pretended to be asleep, even after he left.

EMPTY MOUTHS

The bedroom was cold. Lying awake at night, she could watch each draught leaking in. Sometimes she had dreams about central heating.

The next day was bright, though rain came in fits and starts. Sunlight made the falling drops glitter like steel wires. Leaves had left clear imprints on the pavement; trees held up unfinished jigsaws against the whitewashed sky. Claire felt on the edge of a revelation. It all had to fit together somehow. She dressed warmly and went for a walk in the park, losing herself in the maze of crisscrossing paths.

It had rained here during the night: the overgrown low-lying areas of the park were marshy. Tree trunks glistened with moisture; a growth of pale fungus on one trunk was like an open book bound in leather. It carried on raining under trees, though the sky was clear. In places, the park was waste ground. There was a graveyard for supermarket trolleys at one end, between a ruined wall and a small forest. It was quieter than the park by the Midland Arts Centre; different people came here. Vagrants and drunks huddled on the benches, waiting to dry out. Men of various ages stalked each other among the trees. Hunger never changed.

Claire wondered what she could say to anyone. Why hadn't she talked to the police, the day before? But it was so pointless. Just a handful of images. Vampires. Alcohol. Loneliness. Children. Frost. Scars. If only the monster would detach itself from the people or the background. If only the normal things weren't so broken up, divided. But if the image was whole, none of this would be happening.

She was hungry; it was three o'clock, and she hadn't eaten. The walk home was an effort. It would be far easier to go to sleep on a bench. Stella and Martin passed her on the Alcester Road, but didn't stop. Hadn't they recognised her? By the church, she saw a group of drunks with wine bottles, wearing cheap plastic anoraks against the uneasy weather. One of them was the white-haired tenant with the cut under his eye. He waved an open bottle at her and rubbed it suggestively.

That night, Claire only slept for two or three hours. When she fell asleep, she dreamed of a thin child with an adult face. He was curled inside her, like a question mark. His long fingers tugged at her nerves; the outside world flickered and then went dead. The only light came from the bulb of the child's head. She felt its loneliness, its terrible hunger. The alarm clock turned her dream inside out. There were tears on her face, dried to hard lines of salt.

Monday at work helped to thaw her out; but it was dark before she could go home. In the flat, the odour of yesterday's dinner still clung to the walls. Robert wouldn't be back until late. Claire slept for an hour, woke up and decided to go out. The possibility of seeing Andrew again was all she had to hold onto. It took her a while to put her make-up on; the mirror kept clouding over, because her face was too near to it, because her eyes were too tired to look from further away. Outside, mist had gathered, blurring the image of the street. Perhaps her mind would be more settled if the weather weren't so unstable.

Car headlamps drove cones of light forward. Rain-pools in the gutters had frozen over. The ice was only visible where cracks made it white. *Take it easy*, she thought; *have a drink and stop thinking too much*. Monday nights were normally quiet, but – whether it was the cold or the anticipation of Christmas – the pub was already full. Claire paused in the doorway and crossed herself; she wasn't sure why. Inside, she could see Jane and Theresa sitting at a small table near the wall. Some other friends of hers were among the crowd in front of the bar. David Bowie's 'Heroes' was playing on the jukebox. Andrew was standing at the foot of the stairs, looking into his glass.

She didn't dare say hello to her friends in case she missed him. When she went up to Andrew, he turned away. She touched his shoulder. He turned halfway back and then walked to the bar. Claire followed him, bought herself a double Scotch, drank it straight off. Her face was stiff with blood; it was hard to breathe. Suddenly she thought the only way out was to drink so much that she couldn't feel anything. When there was a quiet spot in the music, she walked up to Andrew and said very clearly: 'You can talk to me, you know. I'm human. You don't have to marry me, but you could say hello.' Everyone within hearing deliberately failed to react. Andrew tensed slightly, and headed for the toilet. Claire went back to the bar and ordered a drink she could scarcely afford now.

He didn't matter, not really. But why did she have to be humiliated in her own local pub, in front of all her friends, by some fucked-up boy who couldn't even get it together in bed? This was how Stella must feel. She wasn't going to get like that. Her life was her own. Just as the barman took her money and handed back the change, she saw Andrew walking out the pub door. Draining the glass in a few seconds, Claire went out after him.

The mist put a soft wall between them. Claire could just see the back of Andrew's coat. He was taller than she was. Would he recognise her if he turned round? Keeping well back, she followed him down Salisbury Road. Huge trees divided the mist, flooding it with branches and twigs; dead leaves were clotted overhead. Across the road, a new housing estate was a mosaic of lit windows set in concrete. Andrew never varied his pace. She began to feel that he wasn't really there. When he turned to the left, she let him dwindle to an impersonal figure. But the roads were shorter here; she had to catch up again to keep him in sight.

Along the Pershore Road, garages and corner shops broke up a line of tall Victorian houses, most of them in a dreadful state of repair. A round-shouldered bag woman walked past Claire, pulling a supermarket trolley full of rubbish. Andrew slowed down outside a fish and chip shop, and Claire had to stop; only his indifference hid her. But what was the point? Because his loneliness could tell her something about herself? She felt sick and directionless; more so than the drink could account for. At least this street wasn't full of kerb-crawlers. It was too desolate: nobody had a reason to be here. Cars floated past, glowing alternately white and red.

Where the road divided into three, a cluster of little factories was hidden behind grey walls mounted with razor-wire and broken glass like premature tinsel. Claire stopped and breathed hard, swallowing mist. It would never make sense. Ahead of her, not much was visible. She wrapped her arms across her chest. Walking on felt exactly like falling.

'Claire. My God.'

Andrew had stopped; he was facing her, only a few yards ahead. When she caught up with him, he stared. 'What's the matter with you?' Claire was shivering helplessly; he seized her arm. 'What's wrong?'

'I wanted to talk to you.' Why was he holding her like a policeman, not like a lover? 'I need you,' she said, wishing she could freeze-frame his attention. He let go of her and walked on slowly. The house where he lived was like all the others, an old tenement building with an overgrown front yard. The number was painted in black on a door stripped to the wood. There were five electric doorbells beside the front window, which carried a Union Jack sticker. Inside the glass, a blanket sealed the room from daylight.

On the doorstep, Andrew pulled Claire against him. His fingers combed her hair. They kissed, very gently, hardly daring to breathe. 'Claire,' he whispered. The mist seemed to run into his mouth. 'What is the matter with you?'

'What do you mean?' she said.

'If you accepted yourself, you wouldn't have followed me. Would you?' He reached for his key and opened the front door. The hall was carpeted with dust, leaflets and copies of the local free newspaper. Andrew switched on the light and turned left up the stairs. One of the flats was being repaired or united with another: you could see through a series of wooden supports into a room that was bare of everything except broken plaster strips and flakes, piled up on the floorboards. At the end of a hallway there was another door; it was unlocked. Andrew pushed it open. 'Come in, if you want.'

His bedroom contained very little. There was a single bed, a wooden chair, a dressing-table and mirror. The floor had an Oriental patterned rug. A collection of bones, more or less clean, were scattered over the bed. Claire took a step forward. There were ribs, a broken pelvis, a small human skull. It was the skeleton of a child. Andrew sat on the edge of the bed and watched her.

Her hands moved above the bones, doing something she couldn't understand. Her mind was somewhere else. 'Go on,' he said calmly. 'Put the pieces together. That's what you want to do, isn't it?'

Slowly, Claire felt her way along the corridor and down the stairs. A wrong step would have pitched her into the empty room. It was difficult to walk, because her legs were shaking; she twisted her ankle and almost fell. Outside, the mist seemed to be lifting. She concentrated on walking steadily. (*I'm being used to make a point. Part of somebody else's image.*) Frost was smeared across the pavements. A car backfired like a series of fireworks going off in a garage. Her mind kept repeating shreds of music that cut into each other, like a radio dial turning back and forth between stations. A young couple overtook her on the Pershore Road, their arms around each other.

The way home took her past the railway line and the park gates at the north end of Moseley. As she stood on the bridge, looking down through the patchwork of trees, a train shuddered underneath. Outside the park, a group of drunks were sitting on wooden benches and the concrete rims of the flower beds. There were at least a dozen of them. She could see the child moving from one to another, simplifying the faces, animating the gestures. One of the group dropped a bottle, reached down and then fell onto the spreading pool. She lay there face upward. Her hands twitched, grabbing the air. Some of the others gathered round her, then started to draw back. A blurred off-white shape was forming slowly around her head. Claire could see thin hands in it, and a black mouth like a hole dug in earth. The image glowed slightly, but it made the surroundings darker, as though draining the light from everything else was the only way it could keep itself bright. It cradled the dying woman's head and sang in her ear. Nobody else moved or spoke. There was a stillness in them like the frost that coated the paving stones.

Then one of the men went to the phone box on the corner. Within a few minutes, an ambulance siren was wailing from the direction of Moseley Village.

Claire forced herself to keep walking towards home. She stared at the buildings along the Alcester Road until she could recognise them. A strangeness hung around them like mist – a pattern of memories and images that weren't hers. It helped to keep repeating her own name, her address, her age, the names of her family.

When she reached Strensham Hill, the house was dark. Robert had gone to bed. Claire locked the door, then the windows. Her sleep was broken up. She was afraid of dreaming about the child. Some time the next evening, she drank some soup and ate a few slices of bread. For some reason the thought of meat sickened her. It was Friday before she returned to work. She didn't try to tell Robert what had happened. They had dinner together on Saturday night; Claire was still dazed from lack of sleep, but half a bottle of wine helped to relax her.

They finished the evening sitting together in the living room, watching one of Robert's videos. It was windy outside; the gas fire flickered and rattled. In the film, a woman dressed in leather tore out a man's heart and offered it to him. He bit into it. Robert touched her shoulder. 'Claire? How do you feel now?'

'All right, I suppose.' His hand stayed on her arm.

'I've been thinking… maybe we should get back together. For a trial period, I mean. What do you think?'

Claire shrugged and drained her glass. 'Why not?' No answer occurred to her. When they kissed, he kept an eye on the screen.

That night, sex between them was more intense than ever before. It was something almost painful, as though they had overcome a barrier. There was no break in their contact. They came together, taut and aching with excitement. As their sweat cooled in the draughty room, Claire felt something pass out of her into Robert. It left her vacant, her senses dull. For the rest of the night, she slept unevenly; while Robert lay facing the wall, his whole body tense, not sleeping at all.

THE LAST CRY

Every night that week, Ian dreamt about the same thing. He didn't know what to call it. In his dreams, the bodies of dead people were scattered on a patch of hard earth. They looked as though they had fallen from a great height. Their flesh had turned grey, and insects were crawling through it. As he awoke, he heard the beating of wings overhead. He stared into the darkness, trying to remember something about birds that ate decaying animals. He'd never seen a dead animal, unless you counted flies. The plastic curtain on his bedroom window was completely lightproof. Ian tried to imagine a hovering winged shape, but couldn't.

In the mornings, he drove into work with the dream still floating in the back of his mind. The painkillers helped him not to dwell on it. The roadway was pale and scoured, gleaming with rain. At his office on the seventh floor, he stared at the black and red graphics on his screen and tried not to think about Tony. It was over: the hospital visits, the two days of compassionate leave, the cremation. Now it was time to be working again. Ian had no complaints against Neotechnic, his employers. It wasn't their fault that so much seemed to be missing.

As he designed and modified page after page of complex engineering plans, his eyes searched for the darkness behind the screen.

It was while browsing through an online thesaurus in his lunch break that he found the word *carrion*. At once, he knew that was his dream. And he knew it had to do with Tony, though his lover hadn't been among the dead. As far as he could tell. He'd dreamed of Tony's dead body often while they'd lived together. But now he was gone. His *corpse* (another archaic word) had been scanned and rifled for useful organs before being incinerated and released into the city's atmosphere. The process was meant to discourage any delusion of continued attachment.

To make the dead go away. Ian had seen photographs of graveyards; he couldn't imagine how people had lived with them.

It must have been like never cleaning the bath.

His dream changed suddenly, on a Friday night. He'd been drinking, alone, to get to sleep. Since Tony's death he'd needed to be alone more and more; it was the only way he could cope with the loneliness. In the dry, filtered air of his twelfth-floor flat, he twisted across the endless double bed, shivering and sweating. Near dawn, the fragments of his dream had joined into something like a landfill rubbish site. He'd seen frozen grass, splintered bones, coils of barbed wire. And chunks of black stone with names carved into them. The ruins of a cemetery. The moon was a thin oval in the night sky, as if it were trying to turn away. And then the darkness around him came to life: a frenzy of black wings and stabbing yellowish beaks; the bleak cries of a hunger that only rotten meat could ease.

There was no living prey. Ian awoke with a sheet tangled round his head, absorbing his tears. There was no trace of light in the room. He curled up on his side like a child, remembering the black birds in the moonlight. What were they called?

He'd slept with Tony in this bed for ten years. Until the tumours had grown out of control. It happened to nearly everyone, sooner or later. However many cures they developed, there were always more cancers. Radiation, implants, treated food, even the city air. And the drugs. *Iatrogenic* cancers – another word Ian had culled from scanning medical texts. 'You collect words like vitamin tablets,' Tony had said to him. He remembered videos from school about the way people used to die: randomly, from a million diseases, often in terrible pain. These days, you knew how you were going to die; and you started dying early, but it took a while. He'd actually believed there was no pain until those last years with Tony, when he'd realised that some kinds of pain couldn't be numbed. Sometimes he'd woken up and known that Tony was lying beside him, awake, staring at nothing. His breathing had sounded like a terrified child.

Then Ian had tried to hold him, talk to him.

He remembered the last time they'd made love. It was a month before Tony's death. Ian had tried to be gentle, to avoid putting any strain on his lover's damaged lungs and air passages. But Tony had whispered: *Fuck me. Fuck me hard. Even if it hurts, I want to feel it. I don't ever want to forget what it's like.* When he came with Ian's arms and legs wrapped tight around him, Ian's cock buried deep in him, he cried out desperately. Ian had whispered *Are you okay?* and he'd laughed.

Things like that were the real death, Ian realised. Not going into hospital to be numbed and taken apart. It was all in the letting go.

The morning after that dream, he walked into town to do some shopping. It had rained during the night; the pavements smelt faintly of vomit, emissions washed down from the pale smog. His skin felt tight. A yellowish sunlight reflected from the upper windows of the office blocks. The roads were busy, but the pavement was quiet. The city seemed unusually clean.

Or maybe it was just that his flat was a mess. Out here, the wastes were invisible.

Walking down the stone steps of an underpass, Ian glimpsed a flicker of movement in the distance. He looked up: in a patch of sky above the glass-walled shopping arcade, something black was fluttering. He thought it was a torn plastic bin liner, or maybe a burnt scrap of some packing material. It beat against the glass roof of the arcade, then slipped away. From the back of Ian's mind, a word came to him: *crow*. He repeated it to himself as he walked on, letting concrete and glass shield him from the blank sky with its fists of wind.

Back in the flat, he accessed a reference file on birds. You saw gulls and pigeons in the city from time to time, but not much else. The crow image on-screen was a glossy black,

THE LAST CRY

wings spread like a leather jacket; its open beak held a faint speck of red.

Possibly extinct, the file said. It belonged to the family *Cordivae*, along with other vanished species Ian had never heard of: jackdaw, raven, rook. Crows fed on carrion; they were dependent on animals high in the food chain. Therefore, by and large, they were fucked. The file had an artist's impression of a crow's nest: a shapeless mass of twigs in the upper branches of a tree, like a blood clot in a lung. Ian had heard that, back in the twentieth century, a poet called Ted Hughes had written a webcast called *Crow*; but he'd never come across it.

The dreams continued. He saw dead things lying on heaps of fermenting waste. Teeth glittering among the rubble of shattered headstones and burial urns. Blind silhouettes of crows flapping in endless circles under the red sky. Awake, he ran through lists of creatures in his head: *raptors, scavengers, burrowers, prey*. Words and animals were linked in his mind. It was all memory. The passing days shrank like pages being reduced on-screen. This would have been called *autumn* once; now it was just an uneasy few weeks between the hot season and the cold season, when it rained hard most of the time. Ian knew that even if crows still existed, he had no chance of seeing one in the city. He'd have to go outside.

The thought of it made him feel cold and vacant. Outside was disease, pollution, wasteland. Sometimes people didn't come back. They'd tried to make it illegal to go outside, twenty years ago; but that had led to protest. Teenagers had held festivals there. Now they didn't prosecute you for going outside: they just fucked off your health insurance. Ian wasn't sure that he cared. Even as he prepared to go, booked a Friday off work and started to collect what he needed, he knew that he probably wouldn't find a crow. But that wasn't really the point.

On the day of his journey, Ian got up well before dawn. He dressed as warmly as possible, and packed his PVC rucksack with enough food and bottled water for a couple of days. But he didn't take any of his medication, not even the painkillers.

Outside, the streets were already full of early morning traffic.

Headlights strobed the curtained buildings. Ian headed north (or a shade to north-west) and kept going. The city covered hundreds of square miles, with patches of the outside cutting into it. Some of the outside was enclosed by it, but the word hadn't changed. He wanted to get to the jagged fringe across the top of the map, where HAZARD ARFA was printed over the vague contours of grey. Ian thought it had once been called the Peak District.

He parked his car at the edge of the road, just before the giant chain-link fence that divided the landscape into a grid.

He had to walk a couple of miles before he reached a gap in the fence. Like all the gaps, it was surrounded by trees. He was already feeling tired. The ground ahead of him rose steeply into the mist. Scraps of grass were the only colour. A few bare trees and blackened stumps broke the surface. It was like walking on a stone face that had been shaved unevenly, and had broken into a cold sweat.

As he walked, the sky overhead cleared to a pearly white.

He came to a valley where a section of old railway track was still in place; a line of houses had fallen in on themselves, jagged walls framing mounds of slate and brick. A stream crept over the bottom section of the track, ending in a pool that was stained with blue-green algae like a gigantic bruise. Ian pulled his coat tighter around his shoulders. Every few minutes, he stopped to catch his breath.

Eventually he reached an area of forest. Most of the trees were dead, but some reddish leaves were scattered over the ground. Crusts of lichen and moss grew on the stony trunks and exposed roots. There was a smell of decay, rich like mushrooms cooked in wine. Even the sunlight felt warmer here, as if the rich foliage could trap the heat. Ian felt almost peaceful.

There were no birds here; the only animals he could see were beetles, crawling over dead leaves and fragments of bark.

The forest ended suddenly as the ground fell away. Remnants of a stone wall were scattered on the upper slope. The ground below was slick and barren. He paused there to eat his lunch; for the first time in months, he had an appetite. Then he picked up a grey boulder, stared at it for a moment and put it down near the edge of the trees. He walked down the slope, found two smaller fragments of stone and put them with the first.

By the time it began to get dark, he'd built a mound of stones and dead branches that was as high as his knees and as long as a sleeping man. He gathered handfuls of soil and dead leaves to drop between the stones. With them, he dropped some items from his rucksack: letters, photographs, a ring, a shoelace, a paper tissue, a wristwatch. When he'd finished, he sat on the flattened mound and watched the sun set behind a crest of rock. His breath was painful and ragged. He'd worn gloves, but his hands still ached. Something felt torn in his chest, as if he'd eaten a piece of barbed wire. The darkness coiled and twisted in the valley, tugging at him.

He stretched out on the mound, legs straight, slowly lowering his head until it rested between two stones. All he could see was the night sky, a blue-black curtain where the stars trembled. His eyes traced the swirls of the constellations, as if they were fireworks about to dissolve. He'd never seen them so clearly.

He closed his eyes and thought: *The starlight is cold. Why do we have to be like the stars? When you die, you return to the world. But not any more. We don't belong to the world any more.*

Does it belong to us? He lay there for a long time, unable to sleep but too exhausted to move. The only sound he could hear was the wind blowing through the trees like a vast, disembodied lung on the verge of its last breath. Finally, he drifted into a kind of dazed half-sleep.

When he opened his eyes, it was still night. The pale ground shivered. Thin streaks of cloud blew across the moon. His back ached from the bed of stones. He imagined his shoulder-blades growing out into wings. Black arches of bone and feathers reaching into the night, scattering the rocks. He stretched out his arms, drew a breath and held it. The moon fell into a bottomless pool of light. Behind him, trees creaked and rustled.

A faint reddish glow began to stain the metallic skyline, and he saw them.

They circled nearer and nearer, flapping awkwardly, climbing steps in the air. Three black shapes that moved their jagged wings as if they were broken. They didn't keep to any formation: they swooped above and beside each other, as if some invisible centre were being pulled between them.

THE LAST CRY

As daylight painted hollows and flaws in the landscape, Ian watched the crows spiral down towards him. They landed casually, as if he were a patch of grass. Their beaks opened, but made no sound.

They weren't extinct. It was just that people had forgotten how to see them.

Then he felt their claws sink into his flesh, and their beaks stab. Deeper... and deeper, their blue-black wings brushing his skin. They flew or burrowed into him. His chest, his ribs, his belly. Then they were gone. He lay on the mound, half twisted onto his side, breathing slowly. His eyes were open.

Later that morning, Ian walked back through the valley to the chain-link fence. The air was thick with moisture; the grey rocks were streaming. A few solitary people were scattered across the barren slopes, looking for whatever they believed was out here. They ignored him; he did not interrupt them. The mist began to lift as he reached the black trees around the gap.

Through a mesh of hard wires, he saw his car. Its roof was flecked with ash.

As he drove back into the network of roads that defined the city, occasional flashes of light dissolved the windscreen. Ian could feel the pain of the tumours, stabbing and tearing like beaks inside him. He didn't need to check the map: the way home was fixed in his mind. He could see the flat he'd shared with Tony – the couch, the bed, the dusty screens – as if he were about to leave. Or move in.

EVERY FORM OF REFUGE

Rumour is another world. Like tabloids or soap operas. People at work were talking about Matt's affair with Kathleen before it had even started. And once it was over, the same people claimed they'd always known that nothing was going on. How could two such different people get involved? But I could see what had made them try. Each was looking for a sort of missing element: a way to change.

Matt had joined the company a year before, fresh out of college. He was a quiet bloke, read the *Telegraph* and usually wore a suit. Whenever I looked at him, I thought of Billy Joel's line about some people seeing through the eyes of the old before they ever got a look at the young. He had a signed photo of Margaret Thatcher at home. I'm not kidding. But he hated Yuppies and the cold opportunism they represented; somehow, he thought the true face of Conservatism was different from that. I thought he was an idiot, politically speaking. But a decent type, all the same. Kathleen was a newcomer to the company, up from London after four years in advertising. She was three days older than Matt, but looked much younger because she was skinny and pale. She always wore bright, multicoloured clothes, and had a crystal laugh that threw fragments of light around the office. She was vivacious and funny, and slightly wild. But very insecure. They both were.

We worked in the publishing offices of a mail-order catalogue firm. They'd found us a new building in the jewellery quarter. New to us, I mean. It looked like a condemned cinema, with fake-marble columns on a white panelled façade. The interior had been rather hastily redecorated when we took the lease. Once we'd settled in, problems literally came out of the woodwork. We were getting used to finding our desks littered with what looked like coffee granules. So far, poison and mousetraps had achieved nothing. We were working to fortnightly deadlines, with printers who were incompetent and mendacious. It was no wonder, in these conditions, that office gossip became somehow detached from reality. Or that some of us, particularly Matt and Kathleen, developed a kind of strange humour. *How many printers does it take to change a light bulb? Two: one to take out the dead bulb and put in a live one, then another to come back at the last minute, take out the live bulb and put the dead one back.* Stress humour, I suppose you could call it.

Matt and Kathleen often went for a drink at the end of the working day. They lived on opposite sides of the city, so it was easier to do that than go home and meet up later. Sometimes I joined them, though I rarely went the distance as far as alcohol was concerned. They both drank as though they were empty vessels needing to be filled. After three or four pints, I normally pleaded fatigue or urgent hibernation and left them to it. Wherever we went, Matt would always use the jukebox to set the evening's mood. His favourite band was the Eagles – 'Desperado' and 'Take It to the Limit' in particular, songs of romantic longing and lonely survival. I preferred 'Lyin' Eyes', with its deeply ironic sympathy for the betrayer. Some of the current bands had a similar haunted vibe: R.E.M., Pearl Jam, Soul Asylum. One evening, the three of us were listening to 'Runaway Train' and I saw Matt and Kathleen blink away tears at exactly the same moment. That was one of the few times that I believed they might make a go of it: the fact that they didn't seem like a couple might not stop them belonging together.

That spring, the climate seemed to be going through an identity crisis. One day would be warm and bright, the next filled with rain, the next bitterly cold. In the mornings, sunlight coming through the windows created a deceptive warmth. When you left the office, the wind hit you like guilt. The mice increased their activity; and after a week when half the employees were off with mysterious skin rashes or stomach disorders, the management announced we'd be moving out in the summer. Matt and I shared an office on the first floor. Kathleen dropped in on every available pretext. She was fighting a continual battle of nerves with her supervisor, an older woman who'd made the department her personal empire. Middle management seems to be full of people like that. Matt was trying to change his image: he started wearing black jeans and tight pullovers. He was learning to play the clarinet, a subtle instrument I'd always found disturbingly like the human voice.

Kathleen was always chatty in the office, but went quiet on leaving. Then later she'd brighten up again, as if she'd remembered how to smile. I found it surprising that she could promote our catalogues with such energy when she had such a strong dislike of capitalism. 'You have to play the role,' she said with a characteristic shrug. 'I've always fitted in where I didn't belong.' Sometimes she talked about her life in London: how she knew various 'alternative' rock musicians and was friends with the head of a famous indie label. I saw no reason to doubt this. Londoners always seemed to be meeting famous people. Somehow, I felt it was better not to ask why she'd moved away. Whenever we talked about music, or films, or books, I was struck by how similar her taste were to mine. Though she was much closer to Matt, their lack of common interests seemed to create a tension between them. There were other problems too.

I remember one evening when I came back from the bar, clutching three pints of Bass, to find Kathleen crying into Matt's pullover. As I reached the table, she looked up. The tears made her eyes seem huge, like empty sockets. 'It's all right,' she said. 'Don't worry... It happened a long time ago. Can't be changed.' Matt embraced her gently. I walked over to the jukebox and selected half a dozen tracks, taking my time over it, flicking through the track listings in search of some half-remembered piece of music I couldn't identify. It was around then that they started going out together for real.

And a week later that they split up for the first time. Matt came into work looking like he hadn't slept: pale, unshaven, his clothes rumpled. We were very busy that day, so his relative silence didn't stand out; but there was something in his voice, a kind of bitten edge, that made it seem unwise to speak to him. Or even to ask what was wrong. Kathleen came in only twice, to ask for copies of an ad page we were setting. Matt didn't look at her. He left early. The next day was much the same, though Matt attacked his work with a little more confidence. Just after he went home, the phone on his desk rang. It was Kathleen; I told her she'd missed him. 'Damn,' she said. 'What time are you going?' Five-thirty, I told her. 'I'll speak to you then.'

We walked into town and had a drink in one of those sad little pubs off New Street Station that nobody ever goes to. Kathleen said she'd backed off from Matt, and he hadn't taken it very well. 'Now he won't even speak to me. But... I just can't handle being close to anyone at the moment. It's not him. Or it's not his fault. He's like a child sometimes. Or I am, I don't know. It was okay when it was just casual. I'm not afraid of sex. Just of having to take the blame.' There was a lot more like this: join-the-dots explanation, both revealing and vague. She told me her ex-boyfriend had followed her from London; he'd borrowed things from her and sold them to buy drugs. 'When I found he'd stolen some of my jewellery, I went mad. Gave him a box of razor blades and said, *If you want to kill yourself do it cheaply.* He cut his wrists. The scars look like bracelets. His flatmate found him, just in time. Now he uses that to hold onto me. He says, *I'll die without your help.* Guilt, freedom. Freedom, guilt. Matt thinks he can protect me from these things. But he can't, and sometimes it's more like...'

'Like he thinks you can protect him?' She nodded sadly. 'Perhaps you're seeing too many parallels between the past and the present?' That was something I knew a lot about, having been unable to trust anyone since my boyfriend ditched me two years before. He'd worked with me, so I knew about the problems of going out with a colleague – or rather, of working with a lover. Sometimes it's better for life to be compartmented. Kathleen and I talked a while longer, going through the options – everything from quitting the company to going steady with Matt. She decided to take the middle course: meet him for lunch and try to be friends. I wished her luck. 'Everyone's capable of madness,' I said. 'Doesn't mean everyone's mad. It just depends on what happens to them.' She smiled, and I could see layers of experience shifting in her face. We walked out to our respective bus stops, waving goodbye across a crowded street. These days, 'rush hour' seems rather a sad understatement.

I was off work the next two days, a 'holiday' that was secretly a bit of freelance moonlighting. Then came the weekend. So it wasn't until Monday that I found out Kathleen and Matt were back together. Even then, it wasn't obvious: glances, a shared laugh, the occasional touch. Their faces had brightened somehow. That evening in the pub, Matt told me they'd spent the weekend together. When I say 'pub', we were actually in the bar at the back of the Midland Hotel. At six o'clock, it was rapidly filling up with the kind of shabby-suited respectable drunks who work in the city centre and never go home before chucking-out time. The three of us drank several pints of industrial-strength real ale, watching Pearl Jam and Nirvana on the video jukebox that nobody but us was putting money into. When Matt was at the bar, Kathleen said to me: 'I can't take my past out on him.'

EVERY FORM OF REFUGE

Later but still before nine, Kathleen made a phone call from the metal-screened payphone in the hallway. Matt said he knew she'd talked to me the week before. 'Did she tell you about Sarah?' I shook my head. 'That was one of the things on her mind. An old friend of hers who kept borrowing money to buy heroin. She tried to drown herself when Kathleen refused to go on helping her. Now she's disappeared somewhere in London, Kathleen thinks she might be dead.' I shut my eyes, trying to hide my confusion. Fortunately, alcohol is a good screen. When you and the person you're talking to are both drunk, it's like double glazing. I wondered what to say when Kathleen came back.

But she didn't sit down again. 'I've got to go,' she said. 'Sorry, Matt. I'll call you first thing in the morning. That's quite a good thing to call you, actually.' Matt laughed without much conviction. She leaned over the table and kissed him, then smiled at me. 'See you, Tim.' Then she was gone, dodging through the crowd of piss-artists like a sparrow dressed as a peacock. A few seconds later, Matt jumped up. 'Back in a minute.' I saw him walk across the room to the telephone. Because this was a hotel, the bar had a proper BT phone rather than one of those shit portable ones, the kind that gives you no change back and cuts you off just before your money runs out.

A couple of minutes later, he was back. A deep frown joined his eyebrows together. 'Tim, this is really odd. I suppose it's my own fault for being a paranoid fuck. But... there was something a bit funny about that phone call. I just went and pressed the last number redial button. Stupid thing to do, really. And a voice said, 'Blind Moon'. Must be a bar or something. A male voice. I said I was trying to trace a missing person, Jane Starling. He said, 'She doesn't work here.' I said thanks and hung up. Have you ever heard of a place called Blind Moon?'

I shook my head. 'Who's Jane Starling?'

'Just a name I made up. That's all. God, I hate feeling suspicious. Not knowing what to believe.' For a moment, the drunken stubbornness in his eyes gave way to a real unease. But another pint lightened his mood. He was in love, after all. When I got home that night, I looked up Blind Moon in the phone book. There was no such place, at least not locally. Maybe it was unlisted; but who ever heard of an unlisted bar? Then again, I suppose you wouldn't.

A few days later, the three of us went to a Chinese restaurant in Moseley. We were joined by Lee, a friend of Kathleen's. Another Londoner in exile. I wondered if she was trying to pair him off with me; but we didn't really get on. He was a fast-talking, hyperactive Cockney with bleached hair, who worked in a music studio and had an ego roughly the size of Canary Wharf. As well as the palest blue eyes I'd ever seen. The meal was like a complex game in which various dishes were passed around the table, sampled and remixed. The conversation was simpler: it consisted of Lee talking and the rest of us making the odd comment. He was full of anecdotes about the London club scene and the various well-known people who frequented it – their music tastes, sexual preferences, drug habits and HIV status. At the time, it seemed unlikely that so many singers and actors had entrusted their secrets to Lee. Unlikely for several reasons. Afterwards, I realised it was all rumour dressed up as personal experience. Just outside the window, I could see the restaurant sign revolving in the wind: the words TAKE

AWAY and LOTUS HOUSE alternating at a speed that made me feel sick.

Afterwards, we went back into town and visited a number of pubs. They became more crowded and blurred as the evening wore on. At some point, Lee asked me what the Birmingham gay scene was like. He'd only been here since January, he explained, and usually went back to London at weekends. 'Maybe we could meet up some time next week, and you can show me round all the local places?' I assented, though I didn't feel wildly enthusiastic about the prospect. On the off-chance, and following the warped logic of alcohol, I asked him if he'd heard of a place called Blind Moon. Kathleen and Matt were off somewhere else at this point. He looked at me in a way that was both cautious and surprised, as if I'd revealed something about myself. In a different, slower voice, he said: 'It's in Digbeth. Near the coach station. But you'll only find it if you're lost.' He looked away. Over the white noise of the pub crowd and the sub-Spector histrionics of a Meatloaf ballad, I could hear Kathleen's distinctive laugh: a mixture of high and low registers, like a mother and a child sharing the same joke.

Things got stranger when we ended up in the Midland Hotel bar, in time for last orders. Kathleen spent a while talking to the young barman, out in the hallway. Then she came back, giggling and clutching a scrap of paper. 'He wants me to give his number to one of you two,' she said, looking from me to Lee and back again. 'I don't know which one.' Lee glanced at the barman, said 'Well, I'm up for it,' and went over to speak to him. A minute later, he reappeared. 'You dozy woman,' he said to Kathleen. 'It's *you* he's after.'

Kathleen laughed. 'Never. No way.' But I noticed she'd kept the scrap of paper. Matt, who didn't seem very wide awake, wandered off for a game of pinball. I should have gone with him and asked if he was all right. But I felt too drunk to move. Lee was saying something about 'you and Gary, last night'. In one of those moments that's like crossing a border, I turned to look at him. He was talking to Kathleen. 'Stuff being sold in that pub even *I'd* never seen. Cheaper than London, I'll give you that. How some of those kids made it home I'll never know.' He turned to me and shrugged. 'I was out with Kathleen and her boyfriend last night. This really wild place in Erdington. Bit scary in a way. She tell you about it?'

I shook my head. She'd told Matt that she'd had to stay in and work on some accounts for the publicity department. It was all to do with preparing spreadsheets on the computer. For a moment, I had to put my hands over my face. When I looked up, there were rainbows in the corners of my eyes. Kathleen was resting her chin on her hands and smiling at me. As I watched, the smile spread over her face like a thin film, from the forehead to the neck. It caught the light, so that the whole of her face shone. Then it broke, leaving a kind of raw blankness. A complete lack of identity. I got up and staggered away, pushing through the crowd to the toilet. The rusty mirror put bloodstains onto my reflection. I kept my hands under the dryer until they stopped shaking.

That weekend, the need for a drink never left me. I'd fallen into alcohol dependency two years earlier, and it had taken me months to break free. Now that pair were dragging me back through the neck of the bottle. It would have to stop. I tried not to think about Matt and Kathleen, and ended up thinking about my parents instead: their terrible marriage and confused, piecemeal divorce. Sometimes childhood is like toxic waste. It's not buried deep enough to be safe, but you can't risk digging it up again. You never get a second chance.

I don't know what I was expecting when I went into work on Monday. But Matt was fine. In the course of the day, as Kathleen consistently failed to drop in or even phone him, he became a little anxious. We'd both seen her in the building. She'd passed me on the stairs, smiling and saying 'Hi!' without pausing to talk. A sort of pointillist friendship. I wondered if she mistrusted me because what I'd learned about her on Friday. If so, it was nothing compared to how much I mistrusted her. I didn't know what to say to Matt, and somehow convinced myself that it was better to say nothing. At lunchtime, I wandered around the Jewellery Quarter, looking at the old façades of renovated or derelict buildings. A shop was being gradually demolished: only the frontage remained between the road and a heap of scattered rubble, half-dressed in tarpaulins.

On my way through town the next morning, I ran into Lee. 'Hi Tim, how you doing?' he said. 'I was going to call you today. We'll have to go for a drink next week – I'm going to London tomorrow. But I'm meeting Kathleen for lunch today. Why don't you join us?' I said I'd speak to Kathleen about it. 'See you then.' The early morning sunlight glittered in his hair.

In mid-morning, I saw Kathleen by the photocopier. The first thing she said to me was: 'Lee said to give you a message. He had to go back to London last night, but he'll call you next Monday.'

I said I'd seen him that morning. 'In fact, he said he was meeting you for lunch today.' Kathleen nodded without surprise. 'Yes, that's right,' she said, and went back to her photocopying. I thought of the boys in camouflage jackets you saw walking through the shopping precinct. How something meant for disguise actually made them stand out.

At the end of the afternoon, Matt phoned Kathleen's extension; but she'd already gone. 'It doesn't look good,' he said. I had to agree that it didn't. But the following day, she didn't come in at all. Matt considered phoning her at home, but it didn't seem likely to help. After all, her flatmate Sally would contact us if anything was seriously wrong. The next morning, Kathleen's supervisor told him she'd spoken to the flatmate. Apparently Kathleen had disappeared. She'd taken her clothes and basic possessions, left a share of the month's rent and gone. There were still things of hers all over the flat – TV, books, records, posters. Sally had no idea who to pass them on to.

Matt spent the day in a state of shock, mechanically doing trivial paperwork and checking through computer files as if in search of some hidden information. Halfway through the afternoon he disappeared for more than an hour. Then he came back with a thick sheaf of computer printouts. 'What do you make of these?' he asked, passing them to me.

The immediate answer was, not much. The first lengthy printout was a series of letters and numbers arranged in groups, such as M GMNI 15.2 and SN VNS 23.1. The letters MRS suggested a woman's name; but then who was MRCRY? The numbers, I realised, were dates in the recent past or near future. Then I saw the word ORION and realised this was some kind of astrological chart. Alongside the details of planets and constellations, a few everyday words were printed: LONDON, WEST B., LEEDS. Then I flipped over a page and saw the words BLIND MOON, next to yesterday's date. I looked up; Matt was watching me intently. 'I printed these off her computer,' he said. I wondered what she'd called the files, but didn't ask.

The other printouts were all biographical information. Each one started with a woman's name and date of birth, then a series of facts about her life. It was like a CV, except for a few bizarre personal details: *First sexual experience; Recurring dream; Things she can't remember; Worst and most secret fear.* There were six of these profiles. All the women had the same date of birth, nearly twenty-three years ago. The fifth was called Kathleen Marr. The sixth was called Jane Starling. I looked back up at Matt. 'I swear I made the name up,' he said. He'd gone very pale, and clearly hadn't been sleeping well. One thought was lodged at the back of my mind and wouldn't go away. It made no sense for Kathleen to store anything vital on her computer. These were old machines: they had no security, and were liable to crash at any time. So she'd installed these files with the intention of wiping them. But had she done that so she could refer to them every day while pretending to work? Or had she typed them out in order to test her memory?

Matt called in sick the next day. I suspected he'd been up all night, probably with a bottle of Jack Daniels. I'd have to call him at the weekend, check he was okay. But first, I wasn't going to let her vanish if there was any way of finding her. It was Friday; there was no entry for today on her astrological chart to provide a clue. Even then, I knew it wasn't really her

I wanted to find. There was no way of recalling her to things she didn't belong to.

By ten o'clock, I'd visited every pub or bar that I'd been to with Matt and Kathleen. There were quite a few. I was drinking in order to blend in, and my sense of purpose was getting blurred. There was nobody I recognised as having known Kathleen. Even the barman who'd fancied his chances with her at the Midland Hotel was off tonight. Every now and then, I asked someone if they knew a place called Blind Moon. All I got was blank looks. Eventually, I walked down the steps at the end of New Street and past the empty stalls of the open market, frames of scaffolding and canvas like boats in a harbour. It was a cloudy night; only a few stars were visible. Beyond the market, the road led sharply downhill towards Digbeth Coach Station.

As I walked, I thought about compulsive liars. I'd met quite a few, and they didn't usually disturb me. There was one man who'd spent an evening telling me about his fabulously successful acting career; we'd gone to a pub that had signed photographs of famous actors all over its walls, and he'd complained that they'd taken his down. I later discovered he was a spot-welder. Then there was a very depressive boy who told me he'd been systematically abused as a child. It was only when his stories began to involve Satanic rituals and serial killers that I began to have doubts. The things people made up seemed to be either triumphs or traumas. But I was beginning to wonder if something else might lie behind it all. There was so much about life that didn't add up or make sense. Maybe we needed someone to take the blame for that. Someone to be the liar, so what we said could be the truth. But what would

EVERY FORM OF REFUGE

the world have to be like, for everything a compulsive liar said to be true? Like I said, by this time I was pretty drunk.

It wasn't until I reached the coach station that I realised how unhelpful 'near' was. In the waiting hall, a few drunks and vagrants were passing the time. An old woman was holding a bottle wrapped in a shawl, like a baby. An acne-scarred boy was trying to score or sell himself. I didn't think these people would be able to help me. Just up the road, there used to be a fairly rough pub called the Barrel Organ, where I'd gone to see local bands play bad rock and have plastic glasses thrown at them. Now it was an upmarket Irish tavern, repainted in green. Everything around here changed hands before long: shops, pubs, offices, warehouses. According to rumour, the National Front met here in an unmarked building. These tall brick façades, blackened by heavy traffic, looked capable of concealing more or less anything. What could I do? I retreated into the Irish pub for a quick half, then wandered down a side-street, found another pub and repeated the process.

It was darker here; the buildings were older, and a series of low bridges (presumably for local goods trains, and presumably defunct) made the streets look like the view through a bad pair of binoculars. Through the windows of derelict houses, I could see piles of rusty scaffolding. I walked at random until I found another pub. It was almost empty; the barman was putting chairs on the tables, but he let me have a pint of Bass. There was an outside toilet behind the pub: a tiled wall with a trench set in concrete, no running water.

After that, for a while I didn't know where I was. As my head slowly cleared, I realised there was nothing about Kathleen that couldn't be explained as mental disturbance. So well hidden that it drew other people in. The thought was quite a relief. No doubt she'd had a bad childhood. That seemed obvious. I didn't want to think about my own. Not now. It was time to head back towards New Street, assuming that I still had enough money for a taxi. What road was this?

At the corner, an old-fashioned nameplate was fixed to the wall. But it had apparently been sprayed black. I could just see the letters standing out from the plate, but there wasn't enough light to read them. Then I realised it wasn't a street sign at all, but a blank disc with words embossed in it. A fire escape led up to an unmarked door; above it, there were two lit windows. I reached up to trace the letters on the sign.

When I knocked at the door, it opened. The interior was a café with black leather seats and gentle lighting. Photographs with mirrored surfaces were scattered over the walls. There were several tables, each with a group of people engaged in quiet conversation. What I had at first taken for music was, in fact, the sound of their voices echoing and overlapping like waves on a rocky shore. I bought a cup of coffee and sipped it. My head felt strangely clear. A man at the nearest table caught my eye and pointed to an empty seat. I sat down gratefully, though something about the light made these people look wrong. They had the fixed stares and jerky movements of people suffering from a chronic lack of sleep.

Their conversation drifted around me, words rising into focus and falling again. I kept my eyes on my coffee; its surface was cloudy with steam. 'Kathleen is changing trains,' a woman said. 'There's no choice. The timetable is set.' There was a mutter of agreement. Someone else added: 'She always travels light. With a background like hers, who can blame her? She never had a childhood. That's why she couldn't keep the baby.' The discussion continued. I looked around the table. Even close up, these people seemed unreal. Their faces were half in shadow; I could see pale skin stretched over frames of bone. They all wore the same clothes, made from something like felt; it rustled as their hands moved. They were still talking about Kathleen. Were they rehearsing her script or putting her case? The café was like a film set. But it was also like a courtroom.

By the time I'd finished my coffee, the narrative had changed. They were talking about Jane and her life in Newcastle. 'Her boyfriend beats her up when he's drunk. There are stitches in the left side of her forehead, like silver in a broken rock. She tells people she was mugged.' *Come on*, I thought. *You can do better than that.* As if I'd spoken out loud, they all turned to face me. I saw edges of bone glinting through dry flesh. The man sitting next to me put his hand on my arm. 'Do you want to be someone else?'

'No,' I said. But they could tell I was lying.

THE HARD COPY

It was a photo in the local paper reminded me of him. Some minor rock band, playing in Coventry. Their singer was a Scottish lad with spiky hair and narrow, sceptical eyes. I bought a ticket to see them. But when I got to the club and saw the queue halfway down the road, nobody as much as half my age, I bottled out. It's no good being a voyeur if people are watching you. I went home and thought about Paul. Weeks later, I saw the band on Jools Holland's programme. Thought they were a bit derivative.

I'd half-known Paul for years before we became friends, if that's the word. He was in the year below me at the grammar school. A thin, dark-haired boy who never made much of an impression. We came from opposite sides of the town. He was from South Leamington, downriver, where the factory workers and students lived. I was from the north side, where only posh bastards could afford houses. In spite of which, he was always carrying books, his uniform clean and fresh; whereas I smoked and fought and hung around with troublemakers. Perhaps we were both looking for something beyond ourselves.

I left the school at sixteen to work in a newspaper office, while he stayed to take A-levels. What had been a prison for me was his narrow road to freedom. But books couldn't change the reality we lived in. I realised that one chilly March evening, walking home from work through the little park next to the Pump Rooms. The bandstand was usually occupied by teenage couples or pre-teen boys sharing contraband cigarettes. But tonight there was nobody there. Only a small heap of bloodstained clothes and torn paper, underneath which something was trying to move.

As night fell, I sat and watched him. His face was a blur. His voice was a whisper. All he seemed able to do was mime the violence that had been inflicted on him. He spat blood and wept in the sodium light. The fact that he'd lost himself, but was still alive, turned me on so much it hurt. I spat on a tissue and wiped his face. It didn't matter who'd fucked him up or why. Standard Leamington stuff, nobody gave it a second thought. I wasn't interested in Paul's attackers: only in the work of art they'd created.

'Come back with me,' I said. 'My flat's just the other side of the station.' Paul said nothing. His shirt and blazer were torn, but they covered him well enough. My flat was a couple of whitewashed rooms above a shop. I poured him a bath and helped him get into it. He'd been punched and kicked around, but nothing was broken. His pale skin was already showing bruises. He dried himself, shivering. When he tried to get dressed again, I took his arm and pulled him into the bedroom. The moonlight through the dusty window illuminated the sheets of my narrow bed.

We lay there for hours, moving across each other like blind men trying to identify the dead. I kissed his wounds, tasting blood and thin tissue fluid. We came on each other, inside each other, more times than I can recall. Despite his lack of muscles and his damaged state, Paul's grip was strong. His sperm was as bitter as the darkness in his eyes. We didn't talk about what we felt. Only about what we were doing, as if scripting the film that was going on in our heads.

'I have to go home,' he said eventually. 'My parents will be worried.' It was near midnight. We sorted our clothes from the huddle on the floor, getting everything right except the socks. Once we were outside the bedroom, there was no reason to kiss, or even touch. 'I'll see you,' he said in the doorway. I nodded and closed the door on his silhouette.

The bed was a tangled wreck of sheets and blankets. The smell of our bodies clung to it like a memory. As I straightened the lower sheet, the traces of blood and sweat in the pale cloth began to resemble an outline. I could see Paul there, lying on his side, half curled up. The recovery position. I turned the light off and lay down against his image in the dark, hearing him cry out as he dissolved in my arms.

A week later, he phoned me from a call-box. I said, 'Come round.' He was wearing a thick cotton shirt and corduroys. The bruises on his face had dried to blackish streaks edged with yellow. He looked like a wasp. We got drunk on very cheap gin. Paul told me he was going to quit school and get a job. He was desperate to move out of his parents' place. 'Can I move in with you?' I told him there was no chance. We stared at each other for a while. Then our mouths were together and our hands were pulling at each other's clothes.

Afterwards, I didn't feel like talking. Paul took the hint and left. I drank some more gin, then went back into the bedroom. His shadow was still drying on the pale sheet. This time he was on his back, legs spread, one arm reaching up to the pillow. I could see him drifting there, a snapshot of relief and peace. Later, I pinned the sheet to my wall and let him watch me sleep.

It was the mid-sixties. We were the generation who embraced free love, drugs and anarchism. But not here. Not in this municipal spa town with its statue of Queen Victoria and its fussy little tea-shops. Here, the sixties were just another phase of the fifties.

One evening that spring, I was out with some mates from the newspaper when I saw Paul in a Milverton pub. Underage drinking was nothing unusual in those days. I ignored him completely. He didn't seem to mind. We moved on before long. I glanced back and saw him by the jukebox, reading the list of tracks. His shadow on the glass reached out to me. That night, after five or six pubs, our gang wandered down into South Leamington in search of a few prostitutes. I pretended to be more drunk than I was, so they'd go on without me. It worked, but simulating nausea led me to throw up over the side of the bridge. I stared down into the murky, yellowish river and saw myself reflected in its slowness, its lack of clarity.

Our paths crossed every week or so, linked but not together. He'd phone or wait for me in the park. Once I saw him walking up Brunswick Street, past the cemetery and the new housing estates; I followed him for half an hour before deciding to say hello. Somehow the coldness of school stayed with us. The not talking thing. I didn't like to touch him unless we were about to make love. In all, I collected fourteen images of him on my bedsheets. A fortnight of passion, like a shared holiday spread over a few months of occasional contact.

The last time was in early summer. Paul was in a bad state of nerves. He'd left his parents' house and moved in with a middle-aged man who ran a garage on the riverside industrial estate. 'He treats me like a houseboy. Someone to fetch and carry for him. I wouldn't mind, but he ignores me half the time. Sometimes I just have to get out, walk on my own.' For the first time, I began to feel some kind of concern for Paul. I made him a sandwich and we talked. But it wasn't long before we were in bed again. 'Don't mark me,' he said as I undressed him. He was marked already. I knelt before him, giving him the chance to dominate and hiding my face from his still, questioning eyes.

A few weeks after that, I saw him out with his master. Simon was a short, heavy-set man with a faintly irritable air. He smoked continually. Paul was subdued. He walked just behind the older man, keeping in his field of vision. They passed me coming up Radford Road, towards the bridge. Paul glanced away from me. Even when I was behind them, he didn't look back.

That summer was long and overcast. A series of rainstorms made the Leam overflow its banks, flooding out the roads and shops around the train station. The smell of decaying river mud lay underneath the smells of petrol and ozone. I started seeing a girl from the newspaper office, Lisa.

It was a comfort.

She wasn't there the night I was woken by my doorbell at three in the morning. The shock of electric light made a torn shadow dance in front of my eyes as I crept down the uncarpeted stairs. The street was coated with moonlight. He was standing on the doorstep, out of breath. I couldn't see his face clearly.

'I need a place to stay,' he said. 'At least for tonight. Will you help me?' A smell of smoke clung to his scruffy clothes. Not tobacco smoke. We were sitting on opposite sides of the kitchen table. It was a warm night, but he was shivering. There was a streak of something dark on his left sleeve, Oil, or ash. Another smudge on his cheek, like a bruise.

I shook my head. 'You can't stay here.' He stared at me. His face was very pale. I looked around the kitchen and saw newspaper headlines, mugshots that a sub-editor would choose for their blank criminal stares. 'I'm sorry. You've been here before. Your fingerprints are on everything.' *Including you*, his eyes said. 'It's too dangerous. I'm sorry. Better if you get an early start.'

He looked at the table. We sat like that for a few minutes. Then he said: 'Daybreak? The morning shift. I won't stand out so much then.'

'Okay.' I made some coffee, poured a drop of whisky in it. I got some canned meat from the kitchen, but he wasn't hungry. I didn't want to ask him what had happened. 'Is Simon after you?' I said. He shook his head. As the first tremor of daylight stirred behind the curtains, I took two crumpled tenners from my wallet – all the cash I had – and put them on the table in front of him. He paused, then slowly picked them up.

I wanted to kiss him then. I wanted to take him into the bedroom and caress him until his semen filled my mouth and his cries filled my head. But we didn't touch again. When it was nearly daylight outside, he stood up and put his jacket on. 'Good luck,' I said.

'And you.' I sat there, listening to his footsteps on the staircase. The closing of the front door was only just audible. I decided to make some more coffee and go into work early. But I couldn't move. Work meant seeing the early morning news and knowing what he'd done. Worse, it meant losing the faint trace of smoke that still hung in the bright air.

The next two decades were pretty uneventful. At least if you lived in Warwickshire. I moved from journalism to printing, bought a new flat just outside Leamington, got married. I'm not sure what stopped me leaving. Family, memories, the security of the familiar. Paul was a part of that. Not that I thought he'd come back – I just could never let go of things. My wife said I was like a canal: whatever got into me stayed there and couldn't be dredged out. Our marriage only lasted four years. It wasn't a cover: I just didn't want to be alone. These days, it's all I want.

One chilly morning in March 1992, a few weeks before an election that changed nothing, a small package dropped through my letterbox. It was wrapped in brown paper and masking tape. When I eventually got it open, there was nothing there but a photo and some kind of dried-out insect. The photo was black and white, fairly old. Despite the fading and the lack of focus, I recognised him at once. He was standing in a park, gazing past the photographer at something in the distance. The trees around him were not much more than shadows. It was early evening. He looked about fifteen.

On the back of the photo was an address in Kenilworth, barely ten miles away, and a date: the next Friday, 6 p.m. Something about the date seemed familiar, but I couldn't place it. The dead insect was a grub, but made of some dark material, almost like wood. How could a larva have a shell? Then I realised. It was a pupa, unhatched, its jointed tail dried into a permanent question-mark. It was so light that a breath could blow it off my hand. There was no point taking it apart: there was nothing there but dust.

The bus to Kenilworth took less than half an hour. Could he really have lived here all these years? If not, how did he know my address? Or had someone else known about us? Surely not his parents. Was this some kind of setup? As I got off the bus in the surprisingly modern-looking centre of the old village, I felt like everyone was watching me. The exposure I'd given up so much to prevent. Twilight reduced the trees along a steep avenue to iron silhouettes, like bars. Suddenly I knew what the date meant. The twenty-fifth anniversary of the first time we'd slept together. And six o'clock was the time I'd found him lying on the bandstand, his face dark with blood.

My copy of the A–Z map was out of date, but these streets hadn't changed in a long time. I turned off the avenue into a road of thin Victorian houses, leaded windows framed by iron scrollwork. The address said number 43. Confused, I checked the numbers on either side, then re-read the back of the photo. Number 43 was derelict. The curtained windows were heavily coated with dust; the doorway was boarded up. Then I noticed that a side window next to the door had been removed, leaving a black rectangle of empty space. Was this an assignation, not a visit? We'd never done that in the old days. But there was a first time for everything.

It looked like no one had lived here for a while. The carpet had mostly rotted away, and the wallpaper felt soft and tacky. Gaps in the roof striped the bare staircase with daylight. I walked slowly up to the first floor. Damp had painted a forest in the hallway. The bedroom contained a rusty, narrow frame. On a cabinet, a mirror reflected a blur of light from the window. Something was moving behind the wall, tapping. As if dislodged like a sudden fall of snow, a shadow peeled itself from the wall and floated towards me. I felt a brittle mouth scratch against mine, paper fingers touching my neck. I turned away, shivering. Another shadow worked loose from the ceiling above the bed and fell on me. A deeper kiss. Muscles stirring against mine. A brief pressure at my crotch. Then nothing.

Another shadow embraced me in the hallway, loosening my shirt. In the mildewed cell of the bathroom, I felt a shapeless hand run its broken nails down my spine. By the time I'd gone back down the stairs, I was naked. It was Paul every time. Negatives, burnt-out shells of desire and tenderness. I counted them: fourteen moments of contact. Fourteen shadows. I ended up in the bedroom again, weeping as I came into a mouth of dust and lifeless tissue. It was night outside.

Slowly, more by touch than the hints of moonlight, I put on my clothes. This wasn't where Paul had lived. It was the house we could have shared. But there was no reason to stay.

Things are different now. I watch TV, read magazines, know that the rules have changed. But what's inside can be harder to change than laws and taboos. Back in the late 1980s, a Warwickshire councillor declared: 'It is not a matter of prejudice. We are trying to get back to the time when, if this kind of thing happened, it happened out of sight and out of mind.' But out of sight and out of mind is not alive. Whatever. It's all in the past now. Only a collection of stills.

That photograph of Paul was the starting point. Over the fourteen years since then, I've collected thousands of photos and sketches. Teenage boys and adult men, clothed and naked, aroused and dormant. Mostly from private collections, old black-and-white snapshots, yellowed at the edges. Somehow, I never lose hope that I'll find another image of him. Not brittle and dried out like I am now, but as he was then. Newly awake, open to a love that never came and bodies that came all too easily.

But I'm no more in love with the memory of Paul than I was with the real boy. What I'm in love with is memory itself. Can you honestly say that you're any different? We never give up trying to pin down the essence of life: a dried pupa, a stained tissue. To make it permanent. And then make it live again.

FACE DOWN

It must have been February, the first time I saw the boy in the canal. The snow had melted by then, and the water wasn't frozen any more. I looked down from the bridge and he was lying about ten yards away, quite near the bank. The body must have been floating, because I couldn't see anything holding it up. It was late evening; the streetlamps reflected on the black water.

I ran down the metal steps to the towpath. It was very quiet and still down there. He looked about eighteen, but it was hard to be sure because he was lying face down in the water. I leaned over, but was afraid of falling in if I reached out far enough to touch the body. He wasn't breathing as far as I could tell. There were no ripples on the canal surface.

By then, I'd been living in Tyseley for about six weeks. I'd bought a flat that was cheap because it was on the main road. For peace and quiet, instead of staying in, I walked around the area. Most of the young people went to the Acocks Green pubs a mile away, so the streets were nearly empty at night. Every time I crossed the bridge over the Grand Union Canal, I used to stop and look down. The long straight ribbon of darkness, flanked by narrow trees, always made me feel calm because it never changed. It wouldn't leave or fall apart.

The boy was wearing jeans and a shirt, soaked through from the canal. His hair was dark. He could have been white or Asian; in the sodium light, without seeing his face, it was hard to tell. I wondered if he'd fallen or been thrown off the canal bank, if he'd drowned or already been dead. The air was colder down here than on the street. I climbed hastily back up to the bridge. There was no one around; the factories and workshops were all closed. I ran to the nearest phone box, near Tyseley Station, and called the police.

An hour later, I was at home when the doorbell rang. Two policemen were standing on the doorstep. They came in and told me no body had been found in the canal near the Kings Road bridge. Was I sure where I'd seen it? Had I had a drink beforehand? I told them someone must have removed the body. They took a detailed statement from me, then warned me that wasting police time was a criminal offence. It wasn't the easiest of meetings.

The next evening, I stayed at home. The one after that, I went into the city centre after work and got drunk, then walked home singing protest songs and as much of 'The Internationale' as I could remember from my childhood. It wasn't until the weekend that I crossed the Grand Union Canal again. This time I was walking the other way, towards the Swan Centre. The sky was cloudy; the pavements were dark from the afternoon rain. I got to the bridge and looked down, wondering if I'd somehow dreamt the body in the water. A breath locked in my throat.

He was there again. Further from the bridge and closer to the bank than the last time. I walked carefully down the steps, biting my lip to make sure I was awake. There was no blurring of details, no sense of unreality. It was the same boy. Floating in the black water, face down, his arms trailing below the surface. He was just within reach. I knelt down on the towpath and stretched out a hand, touched the waterlogged shoulder of his jacket. The chill bit into my fingers.

How long had he been in the water for? There was no smell of decay, but he'd obviously been dead for a while. I pulled my hand away; the cloth stuck to my fingers, then tore free. My whole arm felt stiff with cold. I could see tiny scraps of black fabric on the tips of the middle three fingers, a whitish smear of frost holding them in place. I blew on my hand. The skin was damaged: an ice-burn. Of course, they might have been keeping him in a freezer. But why had they put him back in the canal. And who were *they* supposed to be?

I didn't make a phone call. Pressing my frozen hand against my chest, I walked slowly back to my flat. This district was losing its appeal for me. There had to be something I could have done, but I couldn't see what. I told myself that whatever I'd done could not have brought him back to life. By the time I got home, the pain in my fingertips had become a numbness; the skin was pale but unmarked. There was no trace of the fabric shreds. I poured myself a large vodka and sat on the couch for a while, drinking with my left hand because my right hand was still trembling.

JOEL LANE

The next morning was Sunday. I got up late and made some efforts at housework, then unpacked a few of the boxes still waiting in the spare room. Old books, letters and photos. I needed to do some shopping; but rain was streaming down the windows. Around here the rain washes down traffic fumes from the clouds, and it stings your eyes. A quick trip to the corner shop for bread, milk and a newspaper would have to do. I put my coat on and unlocked the front door.

Someone had left a dark bundle on the doorstep. Probably a roll of bin liners. I reached down to pick it up. Then I stepped back, closed the door in front of me and locked it. I stood there for several minutes, shaking. Perhaps I'd imagined the chill it had sent through my feet, but there was no mistaking the soaked black jacket and the dull, matted hair. This was my chance to turn him over and see his face; but I couldn't make myself open the door. Suddenly, the flat seemed intolerably cold. I lit the gas fire and started to run a bath. Lunch could wait. I was too tired to get anything done today.

As the bath filled, I undressed and put the radio on. News, most of it bad, then Debussy. Steam drifted through from the bathroom. I thought of Carol, my last girlfriend: how she and I had stood together in the shower for a long time, soaping each other, before we went to bed. How had we lost that? Feeling close to tears, I turned the music up, found a big fluffy towel and went into the bathroom. The boy was lying face down in the bath, water running onto the back of his head. The water around him was freezing over.

The next thing I knew, I was standing naked in the hallway and phoning the police. Then a cold terror took hold of me and I don't know what I said, I was like a boat in a storm with its sails flapping and no light, no way back to shore. I must have had some kind of fit. Maybe the police came, or maybe an ambulance. All I know is, I woke up in hospital and I was lying on a narrow bed, my arms held in some kind of straitjacket. A nurse came into the room but didn't look directly at me. I turned away, then saw what was lying between me and the wall. The chill gripped my face like a frozen sweat.

I really lost it then. Not too sure what went on, apart from me being held by two or three people while another injected me with something. When I woke up a nurse was watching me, a young black woman with a kindly expression. I was strapped to the bed, arms and legs tied down. I could feel the ice-burns eating into my face and hands. 'I'm not imagining it,' I said. 'Look at my hands. My face. It's so cold. He's taking the warmth from me.'

'The doctor hasn't harmed you,' she said. 'He just gave you a sedative to help you relax.' She touched my hand. 'Maybe your circulation. Have to be careful at your age, Paul. Now you've calmed down I'll loosen your hands, let you rub them.' When she untied the cloth restraints I could feel blood coming back into the fingers, but they were still cold. I felt so tired I couldn't imagine how I'd been able to move. All I wanted to do was sleep. My lips ached from the cold, but I put my hands over my mouth and blew into them. Tears leaked from my eyes: a silent, involuntary release. I could feel them freezing on my cheeks.

Later, I was alone. There were several beds on the ward, and two nurses were sitting outside an office. My hands were still free, but I couldn't get up. Wasn't sure if that was restraint or exhaustion. The overhead light was keeping me awake; I turned to face the wall. The boy was lying beside me, face down. Wearing some kind of featureless hospital smock like the one they'd given me. This time I didn't freak out. I just quietly put my hands on his shoulders, biting my lip to endure the aching cold of his touch, and turned him around to face me.

That was the beginning of recovery. What I saw then made me able to turn away from him. Turning away was the beginning of walking away, being able to carry on with my life. The alternative was to go on surrendering warmth and energy and spirit to something that couldn't be helped and could never give anything back. Yet what I saw wasn't terrible. I can't use words like *evil* for that.

When I put my hands on his thin body, I was looking at the back of his head. I turned him all the way round, and there was nothing there but the short dark hair over his skull, with no openings and no face. All the way round it was just the back of his head.

TELL THE DIFFERENCE

It had been a difficult weekend for Chris. She'd spent it alone, hoping that without the distraction of company she'd be able to think some things through. Spending every Saturday night with Jamie had become a ritual which she felt better for having broken. But it had been a restless night; and a long, dark morning of lucid misery, listening to the church bells repeating tunelessly across the road from the block of flats where she lived. There didn't seem anything that she could sort out; she'd wasted the day in writing a long and deliberate letter to an old school friend, who was married now. In the evening her mood had shifted. She'd taken the bus into Birmingham and walked around the city centre for hours, feeling vaguely that someone she passed might be able to divert her thoughts. In the bus queue at midnight, she'd felt tempted to start talking to a complete stranger. Someone who didn't know her might help her to recognise what was going on. The fear of making trouble for herself had kept her quiet.

Chris expected Monday morning to restore normality; it usually did. Whenever she withdrew into herself like this, the result was the same disappointment: no light from the depths, just a chilly stasis that filtered through her and overcame the outside world. She needed company, if only to make her seem less alien to herself. At first, the bus to work only recalled the journey back to Longbridge the night before. It was an overcast November morning; the window was blurred by a gauze of rain. She'd gone upstairs to smoke, and the first inhalation seemed to jar her awake. It tasted peculiarly dry and bitter; she was still coughing when the trouble started.

The youth sitting in front had hair that stood nearly vertical and was dyed jet black, in contrast to his perfectly white skin. Two small headphones isolated him from the world. He swayed slowly from side to side, refusing to let even the bus's movement register in his private rhythm. With perfect clarity, Chris heard the music start to life inside her head. It was ragged and tense, a guitar fighting to assert itself against an electric pulse. A tall man, his eyes focused with rage, was rising to his feet in a crowded pub. As he leaned across the table towards her (him?), she realised how drunk he was. And then she was outside, exposed to the night as it pressed in with hard footsteps, trapping him under the bridge. Cars ground by in safe isolation. There was a dull blow at the back of his head, then a much worse one, the pain delayed but gathering in force, at his mouth. He stared for moments at the fist held in mid-air, rings on three of the fingers, a vivid flower of blood over metal and flesh.

TELL THE DIFFERENCE

It had happened too quickly and he'd been too drunk to be afraid.

The music cut out abruptly as Chris opened her eyes. The youth had stopped swaying; he was rigid and alert. But what had just happened? Chris realised that she had bitten through her cigarette. It could have been her tongue. The bone-deep pain and the frozen taste had faded so quickly that she closed her eyes again, needing to know what had become of them. But there were no more clues. The hallucination threw the rest of her day into sharp relief. She was almost glad of the distraction, as long as she didn't try to understand it. Late that night she realised how frightened she was. She rang Jamie, but gave up hope of trying to explain as soon as she spoke. It could wait until they were together; his voice sounded too uneasy to offer any positive reaction. It might be worse if he tried to be sympathetic.

The next incident came at midday on Wednesday. Chris had just sat down in the canteen, hardly noticing the middle-aged woman seated at the next table between her and the window. She had just started eating when her neck seized up; somewhere, a machine began to whine. There was a sharp chemical odour in the air. When she tried to back away from it, her muscles refused to function. The movement going on in her body was not her own. Enough sensation returned to her throat to make her aware of what was blocking it. She could only retreat towards darkness, into complete passivity, away from the knowledge that her stomach was being pumped.

Chris found herself staring in abject terror at her prawn salad. By a face-saving reflex, she swallowed a mouthful that, a moment before, had been massive and inorganic. When she looked up, the woman was staring into the brightly lit space overhead. She was heavily built; her dark hair made a V on her forehead, mirrored in the shape of her eyebrows. It was the kind of face, Chris thought, that could make another face if turned upside down.

After that, it happened a few times every day. Chris would catch sight of someone nearby, always a stranger, and then some disturbing scene would snap into focus before fading after a few moments. The images always seemed to be of private suffering: illness, rejections, beatings. Not all were sudden or violent; there were glimpses of loneliness and confusion that were not bound to any particular event. Or there were events no more traumatic than being laughed at, or waking up next to someone unfamiliar. The empathy was so intense that Chris assumed these moments to be real experiences.

It took an extreme case to change her mind: a young girl of normal appearance, but carrying the image of herself as deformed like a maggot with stick-limbs. There was something ludicrous as well as painful in the cringing figure, its attempted gestures. After that, Chris was more aware of the unconvincing elements in her visions. They belonged to a particular type of suffering: they were people's images of damage done to themselves. From that, it was an easy step to what she had thought first of all: they were experiences she made up herself. The others only performed them for her.

Chris found this suspicion more disturbing than the thought that she might be telepathic. It struck at her conscience in some way. There was no denying the inner rush of compassion that the visions gave her. But before she could ever speak to one of the strangers, the sense of unreality cut her off. That was the real damage. She had never been much better than neutral towards the troubles of those closest to her. It was far easier to cry over a film or a song.

What was happening now was too much like what she had needed for months, perhaps years. And how was it going to help? She wanted to tell Jamie about it, but things were difficult enough between them already. They'd lived together for two years, until Chris had moved out to a little flat in another district. They still saw each other most weekends, but that was due more to force of habit than to either's plans. Increasingly she felt unable to reach him. Sometimes she could talk to Jamie in bed, when her tension let up; and she could listen to him, too, which was becoming impossible for her on the phone or in public.

A lot of things had gone wrong after Chris had lost the baby, about a year ago. She wasn't sure of the exact date. After three months of pregnancy, she'd miscarried almost without warning. She still felt as though people at work suspected her of having an abortion. It didn't help that, at the time, she'd experienced a guilty sense of relief. But she knew the loss still mattered. It didn't throw up any larger-than-life images in front of her. She didn't remember any moment from that time clearly. But the whole memory was there, just under the surface of each day, hidden and complete.

Perhaps the visions were reaching back to that. They were rather like being in love – the compulsive way you felt the world through another person's pain and pleasure. Love made you passive like that, reduced you to an eye or a fingertip. She could feel less for Jamie, these days, than she felt for the blurred form that sometimes cohered in her sleep, struggling towards her to be made whole and given a face. Though her pregnancy had been unplanned, they might have stayed together if they'd tried for another baby. The claustrophobia that had made her leave seemed to have closed around her.

The break with Jamie came in early December, when the dark, overcast weather was giving way to a lucid purity that promised snow. The sky was even blue that morning. Shopping, Chris noticed how slow and unsteady some of the older people seemed. It was a more subtle effect of the cold than the massed coughs and cracked lips of schoolchildren on the bus. A few winter images stamped themselves across the patient faces: black ice on crusted roads, snowballs bursting into white seeds. But already she was learning to blur them together, denying each stranger anything beyond an instant.

That evening, over dinner in Jamie's house, she told him she'd decided to spend Christmas with her parents. He didn't seem affronted, though she realised afterwards that it wouldn't have hurt to invite Jamie to join them. Presumably he'd stay here on his own; he never seemed to contact his family in Sheffield. Both encouraged and a bit shamed by the easy change of plan, Chris started trying to describe what had been happening to her. Jamie listened patiently, a thoughtful expression on his rather boyish face. He was a year younger than her, but had the benefit of a university education that, somehow, he had yet to develop beyond. Her account of the visions seemed to go on for far too long, and trailed off into embarrassment: 'I can't see where it all leads. Or what it means.'

TELL THE DIFFERENCE

Jamie nodded and swallowed the last of his pasta. 'Perhaps first you should ask yourself what brought it on. I don't suppose you've talked to a doctor?' Chris shook her head; there hadn't seemed any point. 'It sounds a bit like the mental equivalent of spots before the eyes,' he said. 'Now that you're spending so much time on your own, you wind yourself up a bit too easily.' He paused and caught her eye. 'I've noticed that you're hardly your usual self these days.'

Chris was already beginning to feel it had been a mistake to raise the subject. A little bar of tension was starting to press into her forehead. There was something contrived to his rationality, as if he were using it to disguise something else. 'That's not really—' she tried. 'No, it's all been too much as usual since last winter. Still under the snow, asleep. Now there's an alarm bell. I can see things dying and coming to life.' Jamie blinked; his fists clenched on the table surface. There was an uneasy silence.

'You're not trying to make sense,' he said quietly, and Chris was struck by how tense he'd become. 'What do you want me to do? You're getting caught up in one of your own little dramas again. You lock out the world and then expect it to come and rescue you.' She couldn't see what he was hitting out at; it made her feel like a victim. Their old arguments were taking over in ways that neither of them could deal with. She was about to try and defuse the situation when he carried on: 'If you want to go your own way, that's fine. But I'll warn you now, if you go off the rails don't start telling everyone how strange and tragic it all is. They won't listen to it, you know?'

Chris stared at him. 'You're the one who's acting. I didn't expect some shitty lecture from you.' The more North his accent got, the more South hers turned. The bar of stress was making her neck tremble now. 'I really thought you were listening… You won't let me change at all. In case I outgrow my *usual self*.' *Outgrow you*, was what she meant.

'Well, you weren't that normal to begin with, I suppose,' Jamie said with a mixture of triumph and panic. It was suddenly clear how he'd managed the whole conversation to pay her back for leaving him. Chris stood up, gathering the plates together and muttering something about the washing-up. As soon as she was out of his sight, she put everything down on the nearest flat surface. Her hands were shaking too much to carry, or even touch, anything. Without looking back into the dining room, she walked into the hall and picked up her coat; then she dropped it, went on into the living room and sat down. The room still looked as she'd redecorated it on moving in, more than two years before.

It was half an hour before Jamie came in. She hadn't moved in that time. He put a cup of coffee in front of her. She let it get cold while he sat opposite, watching her. 'Are you all right?' he said at last. 'Look, I'm sorry. That was all pointless. It's been a strange time for me too, you know?' Chris nodded and forced a smile. It took a while longer for the sense of horror to leave her, but when it had passed and she felt able to move and breathe again, he was still there. 'We can talk in the morning,' he said. 'If you want to stay, that is. Would you rather go?' She shook her head.

In bed, he was hesitant; but she encouraged him to make love, knowing she'd be unable to sleep otherwise. As often happened, stress gave both of them a heightened intensity of release. Chris felt a brief sense of reversal, of Jamie becoming helpless and dependent in the final moments, and clinging to her as if only she could keep him alive. Afterwards, he seemed drained of energy. His body curled up, still facing her; his eyes were already closed. She stroked his forehead, struck by how boyish and vulnerable he appeared in the half-light, with all the tension melted from his face. His neck and shoulders were flushed red. Her tenderness struggled with its opposite, the impulse to break away. She leaned over him to switch off the bedside lamp.

It was still dark a few hours later, when Chris switched the lamp back on. Taking care not to wake Jamie, she dressed. Normally it took her about an hour to coordinate herself on Sunday morning; but the night made her unexpectedly quick and alert. She wrote Jamie a short note and left it by the lamp, which she switched off. It took her more than an hour to walk home; in the thin light of the streetlamps the roads were easily confused, and she made several wrong turns. When she reached home, daylight was filtering through weakly overhead. She had to rub her hands and blow on the fingers before she was able to use her key.

The weeks that followed were a blur of pain and confusion. Going to stay with her parents made Chris feel the past few years had been cut out of her life, vital and meaningless like a diseased organ. Time itself was material. Its grains lodged in her eyes, in the crevices of her skin. She found herself angrily examining the mirror each morning for new signs of maturity. As a child, she'd liked watching the Victorian hourglass her mother had inherited. It was filled with dark-grey sand, almost too fine for the tiny thread to be visible as it worked through the neck, linking a hollow to a mound. Now she was the hourglass. It was a relief to get away from her parents, the house and town that still kept her childhood prisoner. At least in the city most of the faces were reassuringly young and unknown.

There seemed little point in talking to anyone about it. When she tried something caught in her words, making them flat and hard to recognise. In time, the expression 'Oh, I'm fine' became a habit that was too painful to break. And in fact, whatever was wrong hardly seemed to be wrong with *her*. The things she felt and imagined all happened somewhere outside her control. Early in the new year, as a little more light and movement filled out the days, Chris told herself she was recovering. But it was more a matter of having got used to the changes. Losing touch with Jamie helped her not to remember.

The visions shrank in turn. Her own illness took too much out of her. Half by effort, half automatically, she became able to screen out her images of the strangers. Their cries ran together in her mind and cancelled out, until she couldn't tell the difference between them any more. There was only a single pulse, no more disturbing than the breath of a sleeping infant. When she looked at certain people, it was with another kind of curiosity: the tension that sometimes caught her breath at the sight of an attractive man was more like rage than affection. She wanted to hold an unblemished, unnamed body, without as much as a birthmark.

A residue of inhibition, as well as knowing that she would be disappointed, held her back until the sense of need took over. Chris realised the anger came from a need to break with her old domestic self. It was a matter of killing Jamie before she was forced to go back to him: no man was going to take her independence away now. But to be with someone for a night would give her a breathing space. Afterwards, it would be easy to cut herself off again.

It was still winter when Chris met a short, heavy-set man in a nightclub in the city centre. His hair was darkish and cropped close to his head. His eyes were still darker, and the uneasy way they moved around gave away his nervousness. As they talked, she watched his fingers opening and closing over his glass; they were pink and stubby, with nearly circular nails. Like everything else about him, his conversation was functional and cut short. Her clairvoyance, or whatever it was, echoed back from him as though he were a blank wall. His name was Robin; he was unemployed; he lived a few minutes' walk from the city centre. After four or five drinks, Chris found herself agreeing to go back with him. His younger brother would be at home, he said, but would be asleep by now.

The streets were still full of people, many of them dressed inadequately to face the cold. Robin walked silently away from the late-night crowd, the clubs and bars, to where there was less light and movement. Parked cars were massed between concrete walls; drunks and vagrants were slumped on dim benches. Chris was glad of her partner's company, though he seemed to take little notice of her; talk had apparently served its purpose for him. In bus shelters and subways, young couples were pressed together, immobile. Kissing might be the only way they could keep their mouths from seizing up with cold.

The pair walked on, not touching, into the real night. Gaps between houses were filled with wasteland; a few thin trees, metallic with frost, held onto the sky. The look of dereliction owed something to the lamplight, which stretched the same off-white skin over everything. They still hadn't spoken when Robin stopped in front of a tower block similar to the one in which Chris lived.

His flat was on the fourth floor. It was whitewashed and sparse, with a few cheap film posters sellotaped to the walls. Robin was apparently able to keep the place severely clean, but not to make it comfortable. At least he didn't mind her smoking. (Jamie always had.) He made coffee, the cheapest kind, while Chris examined the unfinished jigsaw on the kitchen table. It would become the figure of a naked woman, half crouched, her arms wrapped across her thin torso. The face was still absent; it was evidently not a priority. The posture looked too defensive for a soft-porn image. 'My brother's,' Robin said with a shrug. He watched her uneasily, as though wondering how to negotiate the gap between them.

He didn't touch her until they were in his cramped bedroom. The bed was tiny; Chris doubted they'd both be able to sleep in it. The light bulb was red, which made the bare walls seem less close, the angles softer. It also made Robin's body appear childlike, though it felt as tense as something run on electricity. Chris felt detached, a witness to a scene of her own invention. Time had slowed down. The shadow of their bodies was blurred on the near wall, too large for the room.

The sheets felt like packed snow. Robin's body gave off little warmth; his skin was dry and impossibly taut. Chris knew he wouldn't relax until it was over. She wondered whether, and in what way, she'd be able to respond. For a long time Robin perched over her, his eyes shut, breathing steadily; his automatic movements communicated no feeling. He seemed unaware of anything outside himself. Unexpectedly, he drew away and slipped to one side, facing the wall. Could he have come without making any sound? When she touched his back, he doubled up and started to twitch violently. His hands gripped the pillow and pressed it into his face; his knees were drawn up close to his chest.

Then he was still. Chris wondered if he'd had some kind of fit. The thought of how suddenly he'd become uncoordinated ached in her mind like some old and terrible memory. Perhaps she should call an ambulance; but she couldn't remember having seen a telephone in the flat. Then she remembered his brother. He might know what was wrong. She dressed hastily. Robin was still clenched on the bed, immobile. He was hardly breathing. She thought of pulling the sheet and blanket up over him; but she was afraid to let anything touch him.

There was no telephone in the hall. The door next to the kitchen was only a bathroom, the windows literally frosted, dazzling with trapped light. She turned back and opened another door, feeling for the light switch. The room filled up with red like a sudden bruise. It was the bedroom she'd just left. But when had she put the light out? The naked figure curled passively on the bed looked smaller, and younger. It must be his brother. Retreating, she knocked on the door. There was no response.

Chris felt a rush of vertigo. She had to be more drunk than she felt. Of course that had been Robin. She tried the door opposite. It was the same tiny room as before, already lit in dull red. The still figure on the bed was only three feet tall. It showed no signs of being alive. She reached down and brushed its tense shoulder with her fingertips; the skin was cold and dry over the knotted muscles. When she tugged the pillow out of his hands, the head lifted slightly on its rigid neck. On impulse, she tapped his pale forehead. It made a hollow sound that the room echoed unexpectedly. His eyes opened, but they weren't awake; they were so dark she thought the sockets were empty. It occurred to her that she was meant to fit the bodies inside each other, like Russian dolls. Her hands were shaking as she put her coat on; it was a struggle to get her arms through the sleeves. All at once she felt hopelessly tired.

Outside, the chill had lost its edge. Snowflakes were dropping out of a starless sky, only becoming visible inches from her face. They were as large and light as ashes from burning newspaper. Where they brushed her face and stuck there, she could feel them long after she knew they'd melted. Though the streets were nearly deserted, Chris felt less afraid than she had on the way out. She found her way back to the city centre and the queue for the night bus without any mistake. There was no longer anything in her that resisted the cold, or the darkness. It was a great relief to let the thing in herself that had cried out in pain at being diminished flake away now and dissolve entirely. With each new breath she became more like the night, universal and indifferent.

Just before the bus shelter, she passed a shop window already scarred with white flakes. Behind the glass, the dummies held awkward postures, waiting to be dressed. They were bald and naked. Chris walked on before she could compare the figures with what the lamplight had shown her: her own thin reflection, whose staring eyes held a greater darkness than they could see.

BLUE TRAIN

He'd worked through most of the day, but by mid-afternoon the pain had forced him to lie down. Three times he'd thought the phone was ringing, but when he'd stood up the house had been silent. Now the sun was setting, and he could feel the chill of late autumn even indoors. As he looked out, the windowpane shivered with the vibration of a passing train. The street was marked with dead leaves stuck down by rain. There was nobody about.

There'd been nobody about, on a day much like this, when he'd been attacked. On the way to the bank, limping a little but coping with the walk. Halfway there, some roadworks had forced him onto a gravel path overshadowed by trees. The ground between Lewis and the busy road was cut up by deep trenches, fenced off with orange wire. Suddenly he'd felt a terrific blow on the right side of his head. It had knocked him to the ground. Sure he was being mugged,

Lewis had twisted on the muddy gravel and looked up. A boy was walking away from him, casually, in no hurry. He must have come up behind Lewis. It was darker here than on the pavement, and Lewis had wondered why the streetlights hadn't come on. He'd seen the lad stop in the front yard of the Boss House hotel, and suddenly there were four others with him. All aged sixteen or so.

Lewis wasn't tall, but he was muscular. The previous year, he'd have gone after the boy and demanded an explanation. But the pain in his abdomen flared up whenever he moved quickly, and fighting was out of the question. Besides, the punch had left him slightly dazed, with a faint ringing in his ears like a distant phone. And there was a pay cheque in his shoulder-bag he'd needed to deliver to the bank within the next half-hour. So he'd kept walking.

Fear of escalating the situation had stopped him going to the police. Nothing further had happened. But the incident had left him with an odd sense of not belonging, as if he were new to the city where he'd actually spent most of his life. That must have been responsible for the funny turn he'd experienced a few weeks later. That and the new drugs the hospital had put him on. He'd been walking up the Warwick Road, glancing nervously behind him as he came to the wire fencing and the trenches. It was the first time since the unexplained blow that he hadn't caught the bus to the shopping centre. Three days in the house, working on the Coltrane book, had left him desperate for some exercise. There was nobody in sight. But then there hadn't been the other time.

Just at the point where he was out of sight of the road, Lewis had stumbled. For a moment he'd felt as though he were in a crowd, being jostled on all sides, having to pick his way through moving feet. Some leaves must have blown into him; but how could dead leaves (or even living ones) convey such a sense of hostility? He'd stopped, unzipped his shoulder-bag, and searched frantically through the pockets. No passport. No medical card. How could he identify himself? What if he were caught without his papers? He'd started to run, despite the stabs of pain in the pit of his stomach.

On the edge of the shopping centre, he'd stopped again. The pain was blurring his vision. The number 11 bus was veering around the traffic island, and the hard white light in its windows reminded him of the hospital. What was he thinking? He'd always lived in this country, only left it for working trips and holidays. He owned the house where he'd lived the past nine years. Why would anyone want to check his passport? He found himself laughing – coldly, as if at a former friend he no longer respected. *What are you like?*

The bedroom was dark now, making the twilight in the window seem paler. He could hear another train going past. Another day nearly over. Or traditionally, just begun. Tonight was Rosh Hashanah. Not that he greatly cared. His parents would have stopped working, prepared a special meal, lit candles. It had depressed him as a child, angered him as a teenager. At some point in his early adult life, he'd crossed the dividing line between not observing and not believing. There was something in his disbelief that both his parents had respected, a clarity. It was like a reverse prayer: *I don't believe in the truth of the prophets. In the reward and punishment hereafter. In the resurrection of the dead.*

At some level, too, he hadn't really believed in death. Not as something that could really happen to people he loved, people who were not even old. That had changed, of course. First his parents, then half of his friends. His first wife. No, he didn't see why that was evidence of a providential God. Strangely, or perhaps not, his own situation wasn't nearly as distressing to him. The doctor had told him he had between six months and three years, depending on how well he took care of himself. The main thing that distressed him was the prospect of having to put his affairs in order. It had always required an exceptional effort for Lewis to tidy the heaps of music papers on his living-room carpet. He'd only do it if someone was coming round. Now he had decades of unfinished business to sort out. He didn't know for whose benefit. He didn't know where to start.

The pain made him restless. He swallowed some pills, poured himself a dry sherry to take away the taste. While waiting for them to take effect, he checked the fridge. Still some vegetables left. No fresh meat, but he had some tins of salmon. All was not lost. He took his glass into the living room and sipped it while browsing through his CDs. Always a therapeutic ritual. A few of the more recent ones had liner notes by Lewis Sherbok. But these days, he didn't play them as often as the classics. He pulled out *Blue Train* and gazed at the blue-on-black photograph, then slipped the silver disc into the player.

The opening horn blasts reminded him of the *shofar*, the ram's horn. The cry of repentance. There was so much despair in those blasts that when the solo began, it already had nowhere to go. So it carved its own path through the dark. That was always the thing that got him with Coltrane:

not just the innovatory technique, but the way his visions were rooted in an acceptance of what was in the past and could not be changed. 'Alabama' evoked the endless struggle in the face of brutal repression, just a breath away from admitting defeat. Even *A Love Supreme* didn't transcend the grime of reality, it just prayed for a chance to do so.

He had to finish writing the book. That was something to hold onto. It would hardly be the last word on its subject – Lewis was neither Black nor American, and his knowledge was only that of a critic – but it would be something to leave behind. His own musical career had fallen apart in the drizzle of knowing that he would never emulate his influences: he could only mimic them. When he tried to do his own thing, the result was rubbish. In order to like his own playing, he would have had to stop listening to anything that was better. And that would have taken away the only thing he still believed in.

Blue Train was still playing when he sat down to eat. A couple of times during the meal, he thought the phone was ringing in the hallway. But when he stood up, the only sound – apart from the CD player – was the passing traffic. Maybe that blow on the head had damaged his inner ear and caused tinnitus. But he couldn't shake off the feeling that someone was trying to contact him. Which probably meant there was something he'd forgotten to do. Uneasily, Lewis went to his desk and checked his emails. Some concert dates from local promoters: the Drum, the Cork Club. More spam: bootleg Viagra, teenagers on webcam. No personal messages, though most of the spam addressed him by his first name. He didn't trust the Internet. What was friendship worth if everyone was your friend, whether they knew you or not?

JOEL LANE

Through the evening, the loneliness grew. Lewis played some old records, read through the existing six chapters of his book, made a few calls to friends who weren't in. Finally he decided to catch the train into Birmingham and visit Ronnie Scott's second club. They might have someone good on a Friday night. If they still had musicians at all. He'd heard rumours that they were planning to turn it into a lap-dancing club. This city was the limit sometimes. He stood at the window for a while before going out. The pane vibrated as a train went past. In the distance, a factory chimney was feeding darkness into the clouds: a black trail against the blue of the night sky.

He liked Tyseley Station. It was a mixture of relic and facsimile: the station had been damaged by fire a few years back, and the frontage had been restored. It probably hadn't looked like this in a hundred years. He limped down the wooden steps to the half-lit platform. There was nobody about. The telephone outside the locked waiting room was ringing. How could that be? It was only used for current schedule information, played off a cassette. Lewis went to answer it, but the ringing stopped just as he was reaching out. He picked up the receiver anyway, but the line was silent. Never mind; he was sure there was a train in the next ten minutes.

From the far end of the platform, he could see the lights of the city centre. Including that idiotic new branch of Selfridge's that was covered in white pills and wrapped, after dark, in a pale blue light. Closer, the oblique trail of smoke was jittering in the wind, about to break up. His train would come from the other direction, but the view at that end was blocked by the bridge. Lewis waited half an hour,

BLUE TRAIN

but there was nothing. The information phone was still disconnected. He ought to go up and ask at the ticket office, but no one had been there when he'd come down. Besides, his gut was hurting again and he couldn't face the stairs. He really ought to go home, but somehow he couldn't.

At least they hadn't closed the line, because a train was coming out of town. Not one of the green Centro or red Virgin trains; this one was blue-grey and looked the worse for wear. Some old stock bought up by a new franchise and used for late-night journeys. In fact, he realised, it was a freight train: the carriages had no windows. It drew to a shuddering halt on the other side of the platform. Then doors opened in the metallic boxes, and people began to emerge. There were no lights behind them. Were they migrant workers? Lewis wondered if, once again, he was in the wrong place at the wrong time. He backed away, glancing warily at the tired figures that were stumbling onto the platform. Then he stopped.

More and more of them were emerging from the train, more than he'd have thought the carriages could hold. They couldn't be migrant workers, not at their age. But it wasn't just the people who were old, it was their look. Grey-bearded men in heavy trenchcoats and black shoes. Narrow-faced women in long dresses, with shawls wrapped around their heads. They weren't carrying much luggage. Their heads rocked slightly as they stood on the cold platform. Lewis could hear the same high-pitched ringing in his ears that had bothered him earlier. It wasn't a telephone at all, he realised. They were singing.

Lewis couldn't move. His legs felt numb, as if the ground were ice. The train's passengers dispersed across the platform, apparently at random. A few of them drew closer to Lewis. Their eyes burned like cigarettes. He thought he'd seen their faces in old family photographs. People he'd never met, people his parents or his grandparents had lost. What did they want from him? An old man who could have been Lewis's father, if Lewis's father had lived to be seventy, leaned towards him and muttered something. He recognised the words *Leshana tova*, but not the rest. The old man coughed into his sleeve, shivered with cold, waited.

'I'm not coming,' Lewis said. He didn't know if they could understand him. 'I don't need... that journey. I never changed my name. But this is my language. This is where I want to die. I'm not coming with you.'

The old man looked away. Behind him, a woman bent over by age stared hard at him. Her mouth struggled to form words, and they came out heavily accented. 'What makes you think that we want you?'

He stared back at her, but already she was turning away. Some of the refugees were climbing the wooden stairs to the exit. Some had already disappeared into the night. Lewis stood still, trying not to shake, until they had all gone. He breathed on his hands to warm them. The empty train began to move away. He watched the blue-grey carriages flicker past, like a single frame repeated over and over.

It was nearly midnight when he climbed back up to the street. The phone box outside the station had been vandalised: the glass panes shattered, the receiver burned into its metal cradle. There was no one about. He paused on the bridge, looking down at the railway line. Then he looked up towards the city lights. They seemed very small and distant. The night above them was pure black, as if the sky had dissolved and he was looking straight into the terrible distances of space.

THE CITY OF LOVE

The aeroplane lurched like an ice dancer with food poisoning. Through the eyeholes in her mask, Belinda saw the stiff grey tissue of cloud tilt upwards and back again. She tried to turn her head and couldn't.

The unfamiliar crust on her face was light, but hard; it smelt like chalk. She lifted both hands at once, and touched it. The mask was as thin as paper, and fitted her face perfectly. Its lower edge traced her jawline. She couldn't lift it off; there was no space underneath.

For a moment, Belinda considered leaving it in place. Then she thought *Fuck this*, and punched herself in the cheek. The shell fractured; some pieces fell in her lap. Others stuck to her face and had to be picked off. Within minutes, the whitish crust had disintegrated and blown away, becoming cigarette smoke.

Simon coughed and woke up as the plane was landing. It was still early morning; they'd had little sleep. Belinda smiled at him, though her face was still raw. He stared at her with the photographer's appraising gaze that she'd got used to (and by). 'You don't look so good,' he muttered.

'I feel okay,' Belinda said.

'That's not what I meant.' He turned away to catch the air hostess's oddly formalised welcome in three languages. 'Like a Cindy doll, isn't she? Only less well developed.' The plane taxied through several miles of runway. Pale buildings shivered as the morning light picked them out from a faint mist. The flight had taken less than an hour. Subdued by the cold outside the aircraft, Simon and Belinda walked across the gravel to the vast Gare du Nord concourse.

They were only here for the weekend. It was business, not pleasure; or rather, Belinda thought suddenly, it was business for him and work for her. She was here with him; that was all. Today they would act like a couple. Tomorrow, as themselves, they would make a film.

The Paris Metro was better decorated than the London Underground, and less crowded. There were fewer homeless people – though you could still see them, crouching behind staircases or curled up on wooden benches, clutching plastic bags or silent children. Between two stations, a group of Arab youths played a faithful rendition of 'Water of Love' to the indifferent passengers, then walked through the carriage with open purses in their hands, collecting nothing.

Their hotel was near the Tour de Montparnasse. Simon handed their passports to the receptionist, who greeted them in English. A tired-looking maid led them up the spiral staircase to the fifth floor. Their room was sparely furnished, immaculate and surprisingly warm. Belinda felt out of breath; she unfastened the windows and pulled them open. The room faced inwards: a hexagonal courtyard, paved with concrete and enclosed on all sides. She could see into a dozen or more rooms, all empty. It was like looking at the window of a TV shop.

Simon hung up his jacket and sprawled on the double bed. Belinda stretched out beside him, tender with fatigue. She liked him more when his eyes were closed. They kissed briefly; normally Simon pulled away to look at her, but this time he fell asleep in her arms. The bedclothes smelt of lemon and some very faint detergent. Belinda drifted into a fantasy about hidden passions, betrayal and an unshaven demon-lover with a face like a passport photograph; but when she fell asleep, she dreamed of nothing at all.

They woke up near midday. The first thing Simon wanted to do was go shopping for clothes. He outdid her in that as in everything, having more money and more vanity. 'Paris clothes are months ahead of London,' he said. 'Every new image gets tried out here... it's like going home with the butterfly while everyone else is still feeding caterpillars.' After three hours of hunting, rejecting, trying on and arguing with mirrors, he had two complete outfits, mostly by Gaultier. Belinda had an embroidered shirt, some impressive underwear and a pair of ankle-length calf leather boots; and a nervous headache induced by trying to think about money in English while making purchases in French.

JOEL LANE

Late in the afternoon, they went to visit the Catacombs, not far from the hotel. They walked through the Cimitière de Montparnasse, where the tombs were like small chapels – through their barred windows you could see photographs, icons, candles. Two stone angels were lifting a vault above the ground. One new headstone contained the perfect spiral of a fossil ammonite. Belinda thought of Egyptian burial places, ideal homes for the dead.

The entrance to the Catacombs was in a small grey building surrounded by traffic. They walked a long way down a pale spiral staircase, and along a series of tunnels underneath the Metro. It was warmer here than at the surface; the air was still, so there were no echoes. Belinda didn't think she had ever been in such a silent place. The walls were lined with ancient-looking grey slabs. Moisture formed beads on the stone.

They had been walking for about a mile when they reached a black stone archway, beyond which the burial vaults started. Human bones were stacked against the walls, all horizontal, the ends outwards. Layers of skulls formed lines across each stack. The bones were grey or yellow, and perfectly clean. Belinda noticed one skull with a round hole in its forehead. Around the next corner, the tunnel was also lined with bones; and the one after that, and so on for a long time. They were piled six feet deep, and at least three feet thick.

In one closed-off tunnel, a stack had collapsed and covered the floor. There had to be millions of human skeletons here – all removed from the cemeteries, to make space for new burials. Belinda walked along in a nervous silence, unable to believe that she wasn't just seeing the same few skulls over and over again.

THE CITY OF LOVE

Simon paused, examining one of the relics. Carefully, he pulled a skull free and held it up. Belinda's throat tightened. She wanted to tell him to stop being a prick and put it down; but she couldn't breathe. Her face was coated with a film of sweat. Looking bored, Simon tossed the skull back onto the wall of bones. She heard a dull crack. They walked on, soon reaching the foot of the spiral staircase that brought them back to street level.

Belinda tried to thaw out over dinner, but couldn't. The problem wasn't Simon; she didn't care enough to stay angry with him. They ate in a large, crowded restaurant where they shared a table with two men – one middle-aged and taciturn, the other young and camp. Perhaps they were a couple; if so, they weren't getting on very well. The younger man tore up bread and dissected chicken with a kind of subtle violence. Waiters shot from table to table with armloads of plates and menus. Belinda drank several glasses of water, though she wasn't conscious of thirst.

On the Metro, a small girl stood alone in the middle of their carriage and recited a scarcely audible plea for money. No one took any notice.

Later, they passed the fairground at one end of the Rue des Champs-Elysées. The big wheel was lit up like a delicate revolving crystal, lifting its passengers high above the treetops and the buildings. Simon put his arm around Belinda's waist, steadying them both. Lights were always brighter and more fluid when you were drunk.

They watched some teenagers on a spinning platform, falling together and scrambling for their seats; laughter drifted from their mouths like vapour. Belinda squeezed Simon's hand, which felt cold. 'Come on. Let's have a ride.'

Simon smiled to himself. 'You go. I'll watch.'

'Why have you always got to be in control?'

'I'd rather see you do it. That's why you're here.' Belinda felt something hard in her chest, like a swallowed bone.

They walked on to the Metro station in silence. She tried to light a cigarette, but her hand was shivering with cold. Simon didn't offer to help. On the underground platform, he said: 'I want to call the film *Foreign Bodies*.'

Their hotel room was uncomfortably warm after the chill of the street. That and the delayed effect of drinking made Belinda feel displaced. She fell asleep quickly, hiding from Simon and herself.

The dark corridor seemed to go on for ever. Through arched doorways, she could see white figures stretched out on the frames of beds. People were crying, but the sound didn't carry for any distance. One door had black paper stuck over the glass. Behind it, an audience were sitting around a small operating table where three doctors were removing a child's face. The only sound was the drip of water from the stone ceiling. Belinda closed the door and walked on, looking for the exit.

The waiting room was a huge vault like a railway station. People were huddled on seats and behind pillars, wrapped in sheets to keep out the cold. At the far end of the room was a full-length mirror. Belinda stared at herself: the thin naked body, the bleached hair that looked colourless in light as bad as this. There was something like chalk on her face. Before

THE CITY OF LOVE

she could wipe it off, her reflection broke free of the glass and floated upwards. She saw it break the surface and pass easily into a white marble vault, with stained-glass windows and carvings of angels, where the rest of her family were waiting for it.

She looked back at the mirror, and saw only an empty frame leading into a tunnel filled with broken-up skeletons. As she stepped through the doorway, she felt herself come apart. The clean bones of others, without sex or identity, locked into place between her own.

It was still dark, and the strangeness of the hotel room made Belinda feel she was still asleep. She got out of bed, showered and dressed. Simon hadn't moved. The smell of alcohol and tobacco lingered in the overheated air. She drew back the curtains, opened the window and took several deep breaths. The courtyard below was unlit, but there were lights in a few of the windows. The early morning chill made her face stiffen.

It was an effort to breathe. Her ribs and stomach were bruised, and the scratches on her back were still raw. Her vagina ached like a throat dry from shouting. It was late evening, but she didn't remember having gone through the day. She knew, as if someone had told her, what had happened. They'd caught a train to someone's house outside Paris, and spent five hours making a forty-minute film. Why couldn't she remember being there, or what it had been like?

Simon was standing just behind her. He was fully dressed. 'Help me,' she said to him. 'Please help me.' He stepped closer, almost touching. 'I can't remember today. We made the film. I can't remember it.'

'That's because it's still going on,' he said calmly. 'It hasn't happened till it's over. We're the camera, the lovers.'

Belinda couldn't turn round to face him. 'So what happens now?' The cold felt like a screen against her.

'Only the wrap-up,' he said. 'And the flight home.' His hands pressed hard into her back. She twisted in falling, trying to right herself. Simon looked down.

By midnight, he was on the plane back to London. The air hostess brought round a selection of newspapers with the coffee and food on plastic trays. Simon glanced at the front page, then looked out the window at the perfect sheet of cloud that held every word or image he'd ever wanted.

It was early morning before the woman in the courtyard was discovered. Both her knees had been shattered by the fall. The hotel staff found no trace of her luggage or passport, and no one remembered having seen her.

Even when she regained consciousness, the hospital was unable to identify her. She didn't speak a word of French, nor of any other language. She sat in a wheelchair and watched everything without reacting – as though day and night meant nothing more to her than the opening and closing of a shutter.

ALL BEAUTY SLEEPS

All my life, I've wanted two things. For a beautiful woman to die in my arms, and for my love to bring her back to life. I suppose it's what most men want at an unconscious level. But I wanted it in a literal way. I didn't want the subtext of Poe's tales, I wanted the text. Probably because, when I first read those desperate stories, I was thirteen. At that age you take everything literally, however oblique and metaphysical it might seem to an adult. Later, I could see Poe's love stories – the ones whose titles are women's names – as complex statements about bereavement, about what a self-help book would call the grieving process. But at the time, I saw them as stories about wanting to fuck the dead and the dying.

When I was eleven, my family moved from the small town where I'd spent my childhood to a large industrial city. It meant a better job for my father, but my mother found it impossible to adjust to. The traffic and crowds frightened her, and the pollution made her ill. She went through a breakdown that seemed to take something out of her; then she left my father and moved to Spain. My two elder brothers became teenagers who lived in a different world from me, a world of secrets and quiet rage that they made no attempt to explain. At school I was mocked for my rural accent, and my academic ability was a death warrant.

There was no park within walking distance of our house, but there was an area of wasteland between the disused railway and some allotments. It had been there long enough for trees to grow, as well as a chaos of brambles, nettles and fireweed. The rusted shells of cars lay half-covered by undergrowth, stripped of anything not metal. The soil was mixed with clinker: the broken, discoloured waste product of a glass factory that had been demolished long before. I liked to hold the pieces up to the light, trying to find a facet that was clear glass.

At one end of the wasteground was a dark viaduct, its brickwork slowly crumbling and leaking vertical stalks of lime. That was my favourite place for after-school lurking and dreaming. Vagrants had left traces there: empty bottles, ragged blankets, the ashes of a nocturnal fire. I used these to weave a mental picture of their hidden lives. After I found a second-hand copy of *Tales of Mystery and Imagination* in a local charity shop, I peopled the viaduct with characters from Poe. Those mouldering brick caverns became the vaults and bedrooms in which terrible secrets were concealed: the dying were hypnotised, the unconscious mutilated, the living buried alive.

I still have that edition. A pocket hardback with a red cover and a few sinister illustrations. In that phase of my life

ALL BEAUTY SLEEPS

I read widely, but only within Poe. My recent experience of bullying coloured my reading of many stories. I empathised with the bitter isolation of the uninvited spectre at the masked ball; the baroque vengeance of Montresor and the abused hunchback; the bleak fatalism of Roderick Usher. I was a right bundle of fun, I can tell you.

But the stories that most captured my imagination were four tales of love and death, grouped together in my edition: 'Ligeia', 'Eleonora', 'Berenice' and 'Morella'. They spoke directly to my fledgling lust, telling me far more about the body and the emotions than any of the awkward sex education lessons we had to sit through at school. Later, I came to appreciate how well Poe had captured the helplessness of grief. But I always understood that in these stories, the man was only the means by which a dead woman's story could be told. The woman, in turn, was the means by which the story of death could be told. The Conqueror Worm was not just the hero: he was the only real character in the story.

It was in this way that I came to a rather different perspective on sex from that of my classmates. Whereas they might boast of having touched a girl's breasts, or pass around a folded-up crotch shot from *Mayfair*, I dreamt of romantic encounters in mortuaries and burial vaults. I dreamt of having sex in a moonlit lake, with no one emerging from the water. When I say 'dreamt' I am speaking literally, and you can fill in the rest of the picture for yourself.

The bleak monochrome romance of my early teens was marred by only one jarring element. Every now and then, one of Roger Corman's 'Poe' films would appear on television and I would feel compelled to watch it. Each film would start perfectly: handwritten titles, creepy music, decaying nocturnal scenery. And then Vincent Price would appear and pantomime his way through a leaden hour of crass, overblown high camp. Don't get me wrong: I'm not homophobic, and Price wasn't gay in any case. He was just a truly dreadful actor. And I felt that the legacy of Poe had been irreparably tainted.

The only one of those films I enjoyed was *Tales of Terror*, in which Peter Lorre turned in a superb performance as a drunken, world-weary Montresor. I watched with pure joy as Lorre chained Price to his cellar wall and bricked up the opening. The disgust on Lorre's face as he muttered *Yes, for the love of God* was unforgettable. You could hear him thinking: *Flounce your way out of that, you grandstanding ponce.* I was myself not unlike Lorre in appearance: small, pale and rotund. Girls were not flocking to my narrow bed.

By the time I'd reached the sixth form, I no longer felt quite so alienated. My academic ability no longer made me a target for violence. I had a series of girlfriends, all dark-haired, pale and thin. I frequented Goth nights at city centre clubs, looking for the kind of girls who fantasised about loving vampires. I listened to Sisters of Mercy albums. And I took my 'ill angels' to the viaduct, where I kept a blanket. Some of them found the ambience of rotting brick and twisted shrubbery – of dead industry and reversion to nature – quite arousing. I discovered the reason for the phrase 'little death': in the moments after sex between two people, there is perfect stillness. You could imagine your partner – or yourself – to be dead. I liked to make love as night came on, and leave together in the near-dark of the city's reflected glow.

ALL BEAUTY SLEEPS

My first serious love affair was at college. She was a music student with a heroin problem. Sometimes she injected in front of me. I have a fear of needles, so I just smoked it. If we hadn't split up, I wouldn't have got a degree. She became ill, went to hospital and discovered she was HIV positive. I said I'd look after her, but she left the university and went off to die in another country. She was afraid of her family finding out. And though she never told me, I knew that she had realised I was excited by the thought of her death. I'm not proud of that.

Nor am I proud of the affair I had with a young woman who periodically starved and cut herself. I still remember holding her in the dark, tracing her scars with my fingers as if they were Braille messages. When we made love, she pretended to be dead; it was the only way she could enjoy it. Sexually, we were made for each other. But in other respects, we were barely even friends. She went on holiday without me, contracted septicaemia and died in a French hospital.

Another girlfriend was addicted to red wine. When drunk, she liked me to choke her in bed. One evening, when we were out together, I noticed that my hands had left bruises on her neck; she wasn't bothering to hide them. As the relationship intensified, we were both drinking all the time and the sex became more and more reckless. I left her because I was convinced that one night I would kill her – all the more so because, deep down, I wanted to.

I remember these women, and others like them, with a mixture of shame and regret. The regret is partly that I didn't take better care of them, and partly that I didn't help them to die in my arms. The shame is a reaction to the two regrets. I haven't named any of these women, partly because it would be unfair and partly because, in my head, their actual names didn't matter. They were Ligeia, Berenice, Morella.

My final-year dissertation at college was on the literary and cultural influence of Poe. I examined his influence on *noir* fiction, on cinema and on song lyrics – with especial reference to Cornell Woolrich, Roman Polanski and Marc Almond. The more I read, watched and listened, the more Poe's voice seemed to echo from the dark heart of modern culture. He had cut down the overgrown Gothic forest to reveal its tangled roots: fear, isolation and loss.

The greatest human fear is not 'fear of the unknown' (as some hapless Poe wannabe claimed), but the fear of death. The unknown can become the known, but death will never cease to be inevitable. The reality is worse than the fear. Behind every hope is the knowledge that you will die, and that if you haven't lost the ones you love then they will lose you. The knowledge is a scar on your lungs; you feel it when you breathe.

I had just turned thirty when my father died. He'd gone into hospital for a foot operation, contracted a bacterial infection and stopped breathing. I went to the hospital after his death. Its standards of hygiene were cost-effective. My brothers and I had all left home; we spent a terrible weekend back at the house, trying to dispose of his possessions. I found a box of my adolescent poetry, and threw it out without a second thought. A few weeks later, the elder of my two brothers got very drunk and stepped in front of a speeding car. I think it was an accident, but he didn't survive to tell me.

Suddenly I was living in a different world. A world in which people whose existence I had always taken for granted were dead. A world in which death was no longer a mysterious dream but a cause of practical responsibilities, a word on a legal form, a silence around me in the middle of the day. Suddenly I had had enough of death. More than enough, and more than I could take. I was living in an empty world, a world of stone and tears and nothing. There was no space in this world for dreams of the beautiful dead.

So I had grown up a little, and cried a lot. So I had finally turned my back on the world of my adolescence. Did my fantasies about loving women to death, and loving their corpses back to life, come to an end? No.

For the next decade, I pursued my obsession – or rather, it pursued me – through the endless half-lit vaults where hidden people made money from the ruined lives of visible people. I joined private clubs where things happened I don't even want to remember. I slept with drug addicts, submissive teenagers, women burned out by abuse or madness. I told myself all this stopped me doing worse things. But it was never enough. I wanted Poe's women, not just women like them. The real thing, not a theatrical performance directed by pimps and drug dealers.

Inevitably, I did most of my phantom-chasing in Europe. The insomniac darkness of foreign cities, the narrow cobbled streets and Gothic churches and all-night bars, gave my dreams a foundation in solid reality. In Paris, avoiding the Pigalle and its Day-Glo meat market, I searched the gloomy staircase-streets of Montmartre for a different class of harlot. The most satisfying moments were not actual encounters: they were glimpses of women who lay unconscious on steps or in alleys, the lamplight flickering on a thin hand or a perfect face. I was more a *voyeur* than a visionary.

In Venice, I kept my hands off streetwalkers altogether. I lurked in the darkest streets, staring endlessly into the rippling water of the canals. Sometimes I thought I could see faces beneath the surface of the water. A slim drowned body waiting for me to bring it back to the screen of moonlight. But I never dived. In the long, drowsy afternoons I hired a gondola in order to sit motionless on the Grand Canal, smoking and watching the reflections of women drift past me. I waited for the opportunity to save a child from drowning, so that I could exact a terrible price from his mother.

Amsterdam was not one of Poe's cities, but it was a fertile garden of dreams – whether sexual, drug-tinged or both. I spent the days sitting in dimly lit cafés, drinking coffee or jenever, or visiting those bars where strong, aromatic hash could be openly purchased and smoked. Then I went back to a room in one of the many cheap hotels – narrow buildings whose staircases were almost vertical – in order to snatch a few hours' sleep before the night.

From two a.m. onwards I paced the narrow, sometimes roofed alleys of the red light district. Young women posed in the windows, half-naked, brushing their hair or adjusting their stockings. Occasionally a tired face would be stirred from its half-sleep by the sight of a potential client. I looked for the woman in the oval portrait, the essence of life trapped in stillness. But after a couple of hours, I wasn't really looking for Poe's women any more. I was just looking for *poes*.

By the age of forty, I had realised two things. The first was that my life would not be bearable unless I found a way to make my dreams come true. The second was that I could do it. I knew from experience where to find junkie whores and damaged, masochistic girls. I knew from instinct how to ensure that they died in my arms. I had no idea how to bring them back to life, but then you couldn't have everything. There was only so much life to go round. In short, I knew how to become the perverted serial killer whom the maverick detective sergeant shoots in the final chapter. But I didn't want that. To be honest, my objections were as much aesthetic as moral.

During the whole of a dull, dark and soundless day in the autumn of the year, I travelled from my home on the south coast to the Midlands city where it had all begun. This was after the privatisation of the rail service. Throughout my journey, I was troubled by half-heard sounds: cries, gasps and moans, a distant female voice in an extremity of passion or suffering. I heard them even on station platforms, even in the city street as the rush-hour traffic ground slowly past.

I wasn't sure how to get to the disused railway or the wasteground, assuming they were still there. The road names were no longer in my head. But I got off the bus near to my previous home and let memory guide me as the night came on. As before, the city's glow reflected from the sullen clouds was enough to show me the route past the allotments, through the tangled growth of fireweed and bracken, past the rusting hulks of abandoned cars, on to the deeper darkness of the viaduct. It seemed that nothing had changed here. Nothing had changed inside me either.

I opened my small travelling-bag and took out two small bottles. One of gin, one of barbiturates. I knew half of the pills would do the job easily; but I swallowed them all, washing them down with the bitter liquid I told myself was the distillation of tears. I wanted to weep for my brother, my father, my mother (alive, but lost to me), the women in my life who were dead, the women whom I had helped to die. And for myself. But my eyes were dry; they burned from lack of sleep. I took out my faded, tattered copy of *Tales of Mystery and Imagination* and read by the flame of my cigarette lighter, until the words began to twist and blur in my view. Then I set light to the pages. They were still burning when death passed through me like a white unanswerable cry.

Her still face was only inches from mine. I reached out and touched the gleaming curls of her blonde hair. A candle was burning in a tall glass holder, set in the crumbling brick wall beside us. We were lying together on some kind of marble slab. I reached for her hand. It was cold, but not rigid. Her eyes were closed. I kissed her pale lips. There was a scent of jasmine in the still air. The third time I kissed her, I saw a faint trace of vapour rise from her mouth. She was breathing. As her head rose from the slab, her face was momentarily hidden by the curtain of her dark hair. She opened her eyes and looked at me.

ALL BEAUTY SLEEPS

I rose to my feet, still feeling drugged, and stumbled away. The yellowed half-moon showed me a grey landscape of bare trees and ruined buildings. A willow tree was bent at the edge of a stagnant pool, like a woman washing her hair. The viaduct was still there, but it looked different – its outlines were more delicate, its arches more pointed. There was something Italian about it. In each of the narrow arches, a candle was flickering.

And so I passed from each chamber to the next. In each one, a pale dark-haired woman lay sleeping. The second woman died smiling in my arms. When I took out her teeth to rebuild her smile in my hands, her plundered face returned to life. The third woman died in labour. She gave birth to a tiny daughter whom I washed in a stone basin, and saw at once to be a perfect miniature of her lost mother. And so it went on. There were no days, only a succession of nights.

I'm not sure when I first became aware that someone was watching me. A shadow-figure, presumably a tramp, lurking in the background as I embraced my spectral brides. He was holding a bottle, sometimes with his lips clasped to the neck. As I emerged from each chamber into the rotting moonlight, he turned away with a shrug that suggested bitter acquiescence.

At length I resolved to challenge him. He made no attempt to avoid my gaze as I approached him, but remained in the barred shadow of the willow tree. He was a short man with dark, wavy hair and a thin moustache. He was looking rather the worse for wear. Of course, I knew who it was. His bottle flashed green in the moonlight, and I smelt absinthe.

'I suppose you'd like a drink,' he said.

'That would be wonderful. Thank you.'

He nodded slowly. 'I have some bottles... a rather fine sherry. Medium dry. They're in a vault. You never know who'll try to steal your liquor. It's not far away, but of course it's very damp down there. And you're looking a bit shaky, my friend. Perhaps we won't bother.'

'No,' I said. 'Perhaps we won't.'

The shade looked down at his green bottle, then looked back at me. There was something of resignation in his dark eyes, but also something of anger. 'I know these women,' he said quietly. 'I have loved them for a century and a half. But they don't belong to me. They belong to death. You can't possibly understand.'

'I've been there,' I said.

'Oh, have you?' He laughed, then coughed painfully. 'Just listen for once. The worst thing about fame is that people think they own you. You wouldn't know about that, of course. It adds insult to injury. Not only am I doomed to an eternity of grief and regret, I have to share it with the likes of you. I can't even have an afterlife of my own.'

He took a long draught from the absinthe bottle, shuddered, and turned away. I was alone in the shadow of the viaduct.

THE BRAND

The park followed the course of the southward-running river for more than a mile, from a level concrete playground to the erratically sloping marsh frontiers of National Trust property.

The river, which had worn quite steeply into the clay, ran through the middle of the grey-green strip. In the dense hush of the summer evening its low gurgle could be heard at quite a distance, accompanied by the staccato barking of dogs and the call of pigeons in the trees to either side. Momentarily all sounds were drowned out by the nasal whine of a jet aeroplane.

Steven imagined the sound as a pencil-line of darkness opening in the sky's blue-white sheet as if a zip were being pulled. Through the gaps some unpleasant essence was coming through; but quiet, returning, sealed whatever had loosened there. He stood taut, rubbing at the sweat in his eyes. He was eleven years old, his hair reverting this last summer from brown to the red of several years past, his face and arms reddened also by sun and exertion.

The game was finished; small groups of boys drifted off out of sight. Steven glanced at the scratched face of his wristwatch: it was nearly eight o'clock. He had no inclination to go home, where the air would be cobwebbed with tension. *The house is a magnifying glass,* he thought: *if you stand in the wrong spot it burns you.* Thoughts like this were occurring to him quite often lately; he already knew better than to say them out loud. He stared at the westward sun until he began to squint. Marigolds broke open over the sky and the grass as he walked towards the park's single bridge over the river; he drew in a breath. The fair-haired boy standing on the other side was looking in another direction. On the bridge, Steven counted the railings like passing seconds. The low water was dark and sluggish; it smelt. Upstream, an Alsatian surged up to the bank in a noisy display of gums. Peter leaned forward to watch it. The bank loomed.

Running in from Peter's right, Steven caught the other boy's shoulder with his raised forearm. Peter fell to his knees and stared for a moment down into the river, then rose to meet his attacker. Taking advantage of his longer reach, he ran Steven backwards for several steps, catching him in the throat with a final open-handed lunge. For an instant the blue was opened up again, but the wave of dark held back. Their eyes met briefly; they both smiled, the game acknowledged. Then they struggled on the bank, the river whispering in their ears, with a rage that intensified as it became less elegant.

Eventually Peter, flailing on his back like an insect,

grabbed a flat stone; lunged at Steven's head and missed; then cried out as Steven's teeth trapped the knuckle of his thumb. The stone fell. As Steven halted, astonished by the taste of blood, the dark hovered close behind. The other hand rose through the sun with a black spear that cut into Steven's forehead. Silence gulped hard on all of the sounds. The burning hand flicked off a switch.

Reality was thin and pale, a wax painting washed over with watercolours. Steven remembered watching two people fight in a hall of mirrors, and himself using the mirrors as steppingstones across outer space, which he had expected to possess stars.

Years ago, Steven used to dream that his house was on fire; this was like waking from that to the dawn and the calm clarity of distant sounds.

Heatstroke, he thought with some justice. He had to get out of the sun (though it was implanted in his forehead, no doubt a black and cratered star; he didn't dare to risk restoring it to life by touching it). Between the river and the eastward strip of woodland there was a waste region; even after two months without rain, it had yielding marshy patches. The grass was taller and greener here, mingled with purple thistles and other thin, brittle flowers. Grey toadstools studded the dark earth.

Steven brushed, flinching, past a ghostly clump of white grass-fronds. Weightless seeds clung to his hands. The smell of woodland grew stronger, and then wings flickered over him. Some deep-voiced bird, not a pigeon, was calling.

Looking for a place where he wouldn't need to shut his eyes, he walked slowly up the slope and pushed through creaking undergrowth. Only gradually did he become aware that the voice was human; by then it was very near at hand.

Was she calling 'Please' or 'Steve'? Surely it was his mother.

Time seemed to be flowing around corners. How late was it?

Waving a frail white stick over the ground as if it was a diving rod, a small hunched figure crossed his path from the left. The foliage overhead was thick, and Steven couldn't make out the old woman's face with any clarity. He must be dazed still; the overhanging gloom couldn't be natural. His own breathing was harsh in his ears; somewhere further up the slope, a dead branch cracked loose and rattled to the ground. The woman raised her head, like a cat sniffing. Her height matched the boy's, but her dress, of some faded grey material, hung on her as though on a clothes-horse.

'Hello?' she half-whispered in a thin voice. 'Can you help me, please?' Steven nodded pointlessly.

'My guide has run away. I want to find the gate—'She pointed vaguely with her stick. To the north and west the trees thickened on the slope, at some point reaching the high cemetery wall. A grass-streaked footpath led that way; perhaps it turned off northwards to the main road.

'You mean the park gate?'

'No, the gate in the wood.' Again she gestured up the overgrown slope. A dog was barking somewhere close by; the sound echoed as though it had more than one source. Perhaps it was the missing guide. He touched her bony left arm and steered her gently onto the path.

'Thank you, young man.' She moved hesitantly in jerking steps, the tip of her stick a hypnotic pale twitching in front of her tiny feet. 'I can't control him in the wood. Something gets into his head,' she complained. Another branch fell heavily in the distance. Directing someone else's movements seemed to be restoring his own balance, but he wasn't sure. His steps felt heavy and deliberate. Every movement, however small, was made as though for the first time. Moments from the fight moved though his mind in a jarring sequence of photographs, all in false perspectives. The darkness of the bruise was spreading over his face. If whatever was swelling in the centre of his mind was allowed to reach the surface, it would burst like a dry puff-ball, scattering its spores to attach to the leaves and webs. His thoughts danced on ahead, not looking back at him.

The fear began to split outwards into a mosaic of tints.

Ahead were the black river and the spinning flat stone. The path hadn't changed its course; but instead of reaching the cemetery the forest had thickened, shutting out the church steeple that must be up ahead. They seemed to have walked impossibly far. The old woman was saying something; Steven forced himself to listen. '...can't live without rain. It all just burns away. What will we live on then?' Steven made some reply that he couldn't hear. Above the path a dead tree had fallen into the crutch of a larger tree, so that the boy and the woman had to step through a triangular gap with a face of withered fungus clumped on either side at ground level. As they passed, the sun flickered briefly through the leaves and what must have been clouds overhead, though the sky had been clear before. Steven saw two sparks in the woman's unfocused eyes – and then, for the first time, saw her face clearly. It was innocent and childlike, though closely webbed with wrinkles.

At the time, he did not understand what had frightened him; and another shock followed so close after the first that it seemed like a false memory. When he stepped back involuntarily, the woman kept moving. At the moment that his hand lost contact with her arm, he was thrown into absolute darkness.

Leaves brushed his arms and legs like tiny groping fingers.

Standing upright in utter panic, he couldn't hear his own breathing or any of the usual background sounds. But through the layers of silence, coming nearer, he heard a series of low barks.

He turned in some direction and fell immediately onto a thorny shrub; it was horrible not to hear his own shout of pain.

After another few steps his arms half-embraced a narrow trunk.

The bark was wet and slimy; something rubbed off onto his palms. Then he was too afraid of whatever else he might touch to move further. A weight struck his shoulder from behind, turning him fully around before he fell; and then a mouth of incredible heat closed on his left hand. The pain locked his entire arm; several seconds passed before he realised the teeth no longer held him. The gate, he realised with sudden clarity: that was the only way out.

There were moments more of insane circles and dead ends before he saw the gate. The vague, equivocal light that drifted through it into the darkness framed a distinct form, taller and wider than himself: the woman's face floated in the gap, its creases as strong as a pattern of twigs. The lips were parted in a silent cry of pain; the huge shadow-eyes were blind. But they still saw.

The river flexed and relaxed. Nothing else stirred in the park.

On the foreshortened horizon the sun made a few streaks of purple and yellow, veins in a tight skin. Blue-black shapes were swelling over the sky. Mist and shadow trapped the remaining light. Steven's body was coated with sweat. He was standing on the bridge, holding onto two railings, his head bent down over the dull water where a heavy form, perhaps human, was struggling to break the surface. The entire river was subtly alive with the movement of wholly or partly submerged limbs.

Protesting faces turned over to breathe the slack current; their eyes were full of silt.

Steven looked at his wristwatch. The hands were obscured by a web of cracks that radiated from the centre of the dial. *That must have happened in the fight,* he thought, and felt utterly at a loss. Images passed in the water flowing between the banks, remaining incomplete as they floated out of sight. The sunburned skin of his arms and face crept with its own sullen life.

He touched his forehead: a bulky swelling had taken root there, separate from himself. He still felt the toothmarks on either side of his right thumb, but no bite was visible.

The shadows huddled around him were the only proof of daylight. He stared into the bruised sky. Darkness appeared to close the river's wound. By squinting he could see that the landscape held the after-image of the blind face, like a water-mark.

The clay-face of the old woman. He knew why it had frightened him. It belonged to one of the first books he had ever read: a tiny black line drawing near the end of the last of many stories. The story of the hunter (was his name Finlay? Finlayson?) who let an aged, blind woman into his hut in the forest on a stormy night; and her three sons, who were wolves, came in after her.

Steven began to walk slowly towards the park gates, letting the memory trail behind him. The park was almost deserted: a few couples strolled or sat by the river; someone was standing on the playground by the gates, looking out over the scene.

Near the edge of the forest, beyond the river, a large black dog and a smaller grey one were noisily fighting; or perhaps mating, at this distance he couldn't tell which. Their barking merged into one voice. Pigeons called to each other monotonously; he imagined he could hear his mother in the distance, calling his name. Could he? He walked faster, and almost passed his father on the playground before recognising him.

'Hullo, Steve.' The man's exhaustion was evident from his posture. His immobility bound the air around him. 'You're late, I came to find you. Your mother is worried.' Steven had to strain to catch the words.

'I'm sorry.'

'What have you done to your face?' His hands were as tense as wire.

'An accident. Playing football.' His father smiled uneasily.

Steven's gaze shifted away to the retreating hands; he

THE BRAND

blinked, glimpsing a mark on the knuckle of the right hand. It was a large fleck of dried blood.

'Listen, Steve.' There was a flicker of intonation in the voice now. 'I'm going away for a while. A few days at least.' His left hand gently stroked the knuckles of his right. The dark stain flashed on and off between the fingers like an alarm lamp.

Steven tried not to look at it. 'I'll see you again soon. I'll talk to you.' His eyes were unable to find the boy's; following them down, they fixed on the hand. There was no mark on it. This light couldn't be trusted. 'Come on.'

They walked through the rusted stile and the open gateway in the fading light; the streetlamps shed a weak yellowish vapour. One lamp had just lit, and was still coloured a deep red. 'Take care, then,' said his father and gripped Steven's arm.

'Go on home.'

They went in opposite directions, turned and waved, then went on. When Steven turned a second time, his father had disappeared into the shade of trees on the steep hill. The boy concentrated on walking as evenly as possible. It wasn't far at all to the top of the next slope, level with the eastward edge of the forest. As he passed the frayed grey church an odd distraction slowed him. There was a prickling on his skin, a secretive rustling like the river but from all around, where the road was growing darker in a rash of tiny, distinct marks.

At last; at long last.

Rain or no rain, the sexton was busy in the churchyard as the boy stood looking at him over the low cobbled wall. The new grave was more than half dug and the sexton stood in it up to his waist, turning over great shovelfuls of black dirt to one side. Behind the grave the sexton's dog, a huge black mastiff, sat still and looked back at Steven through the rain that grew heavier, and intermittently through the darker, unequivocal rain of falling soil.

ALOUETTE

I hate it when the phone rings at night. My first thought is that something's happened to one of my parents, or my brother. If it's my mobile and I'm at home, at least I know they'd be more likely to try the land line. But you never know what people will do in a crisis. So when my new Nokia phone burst into song before dawn, with Monday morning just a few hours away, I shook off whatever dream of unrealised sexual opportunity I was having that night and grabbed it. The phone I mean, not the opportunity. It shivered in my hand like a tiny bird.

The screen flickered. I saw blurred figures moving in the near-gold of a streetlight. Someone was sending me film. One of my mates, in a fit of alcoholic insomnia. On a Sunday night? I couldn't make out who the figures were or where they were. It looked like a park, or the edge of a wood. And I could hear singing. Several voices, not quite in the same key or tempo. The song was familiar, but I couldn't make out the words.

The mobile sending the images was scanning from face to face. They looked like teenagers just a year or two beyond puberty. A blonde girl. Two scrawny lads who might be twins, close together. A short boy with the same stubble on his head as on his face. I could see their mouths twisting as they sang. They were moving slowly back and forth, but not dancing. Then the sender moved back, and I saw that the kids were in a ragged circle around someone. The camera tilted forward. There was someone on the ground between them.

It was a man. I didn't recognise him, but then his face was a mess. The others were kicking him in a slow, deliberate kind of way, as if carrying out some kind of training exercise for the benefit of a manager. The only thing I could think of was that I recognised the song. It was something I'd heard in primary school. Our French teacher had got us to learn it. 'Alouette'. A playground song about plucking a lark. But it didn't sound quite the same. Then the screen went dead.

My breathing sounded abnormally loud in the quiet room. I tried to get the caller's number, but there was nothing. Then I tried to replay the video message, but it hadn't saved. What was I supposed to do? Maybe the police would be able to recover the images. Or maybe they'd think I was an attention-seeking loser with dubious fantasies. I was already beginning to doubt that it had been more than an unusually vivid dream. After all, I'd read about this kind of thing. *Happy slapping*, the papers called it. But the kids hadn't looked happy at all. They'd just looked resigned. I didn't get back to sleep.

ALOUETTE

The next night, it happened again. A different victim, no older than the kids delivering the beating. He was up against a garage wall and they were punching him until he fell, then kicking. He curled up in a ball, but they kicked his back until the pain made him unfold. The blonde girl was leading the chant. It was a hybrid of French and English, in a call and response pattern:

Alouette, gentil Alouette
Alouette, je te batterai
Je te batterai le face – je te batterai le face
Et le back – et le back
Et les guts – et les guts
Ohhhh...

It wasn't so much the blood that frightened me, or the look of panic and confusion on the victim's bruised face. It was the look of dull concentration on the faces of the gang. This wasn't some kind of wild spree for them. This was work.

When the screen went blank, I tried again to recover the message or the sender's number. Nothing. I wiped the sweat off my face. It was a close August night, but I was shivering. I knew I couldn't go to the police. And not just because I had no evidence. It was the call. Like some kind of ritual. It meant something beyond what had simply happened.

All day at work, I was so tired I could barely focus. My eyes kept shutting while I tried to design the pages of the venue guide that was due to go to print at the end of the week. Every time I opened them again, I was afraid at what I might see on the screen. I caught up maybe an hour of sleep in ten-second bursts through the day, neither refreshing nor conducive to work. Luckily, my manager didn't notice. She didn't seem too wide awake either. Probably that boyfriend of hers keeping her busy half the night. A few times lately, she'd come into the office wearing what was obviously an evening outfit and looking even more smug than usual.

The next night, I turned my phone off. But that felt wrong, as if I was playing dead. I reached out in the dark and switched it back on. A couple of restless hours later, it rang. This time the screen was bright: a security light in some kind of industrial estate. They'd trapped a thin white-haired man against a chain-link fence at the back of a warehouse. Two of them held him while the girl aimed a series of measured kicks at his lower body. *Je te batterai les balls.* The crotch of his jeans was soaked with blood. He was screaming, but all I could hear was the song.

As the dawn light seeped through my bedroom curtains, I tried to remember what the victim's expression had reminded me of. It was nothing I'd seen: just an image in my head after reading something. I scanned my bookshelves, but nothing reminded me. Then I lay back down on the twisted duvet to try and snatch a half-hour of sleep before the alarm clock went off. At once, the words came back to me from my college days. It was Browning. The terrible blind horse that Childe Roland saw in the wasteland:

Alive? he might be dead for aught I know,
With that red gaunt and colloped neck a-strain,
And shut eyes underneath the rusty mane;

ALOUETTE

Seldom went such grotesqueness with such woe;
I never saw a brute I hated so;
He must be wicked to deserve such pain.

I felt a surge of anger at the old man. I didn't want to know what he'd done, what crimes he was being punished for. That thought helped me get through the day. I was beginning to notice other people looking like they hadn't slept well. Dull expressions, rings around the eyes. And on the train, whenever a mobile phone went off people froze until the call was answered. A few people were sending texts, but hardly anyone was speaking.

That evening, I had a call on my land line. It was Richard, a friend I hadn't seen in a few weeks. He sounded anxious. We caught up in a perfunctory sort of way; neither of us had much news. He said, 'I'm worn out. Haven't had much sleep lately.' I said I hadn't either. In fact, I was struggling to focus on his call.

Then he said, 'I've been getting these weird phone calls. Video messages, waking me up in the night. Like someone's taking pictures of people getting beaten up and sending them to me. What the kids call *happy slapping*. You know? Either it's some kind of hoax, for advertising or something, or there's something bad going on out there.'

'Do they sing?' I asked. But I managed to pull the phone away from my mouth before the last word came out. He asked what I'd said. 'Strange thing,' I told him. 'If that was going on, you'd think the papers would cover it. They're all over the crime issue at the moment. It's probably a scam of some kind.'

'Or a message,' Richard said. 'I think it means something.'

'You're just not getting enough sleep.' I rubbed at my forehead, where a bar of tension was starting to form. 'Anyway, I'd better go. Take care.'

The daylight was fading, making Yardley into a bootleg copy of itself. I walked through the Swan Centre and out along the main road, past the curry houses and massage parlours and phone shops, to the older industrial district. There was hardly anyone on the streets. I walked past unlit factories to the metal bridge over the canal, which reflected a greater darkness than the sky held. From somewhere in the distance, I could hear voices chanting.

My phone didn't ring that night, but I woke up anyway. What did it mean if the calls stopped? I sang 'Alouette' to myself, the original words, as if that could record over the new versions. *Je te plumerai la tête.* I imagined them surrounding me. The blonde girl holding the camera. The phone lay on the bedside table, inert. I knew how it felt.

The next night there was nothing, but the night after that my mobile's tone cut through the darkness like the voice of an ex-lover. I raised it to my face, heard the chant. Someone was running through a car park. With a jolt, I recognised the scene: it was outside the Mailbox, in the city centre. The lights above the car park had red mock-Chinese lampshades. The youngsters pursued their quarry into the subway, where they surrounded him. The camera descended towards his pale face as the first blows landed. It was Richard. His lips framed the silent message: *Help me.* I watched as a sovereign ring changed his looks. *Je te batterai le mouth.*

ALOUETTE

The screen went dead. I tasted blood, realised I'd bitten through my lip and opened an old scar. There hadn't been a close-up like that before. It was a message to me. I got out of bed, made some coffee and sat there with the light off, looking out through the window onto the still roadway.

Two nights later, the phone rang almost as soon as I'd gone to bed. The little screen showed me a tough-looking lad coming out of a pub on an estate – Lee Bank, I thought, from the boarded windows of the nearest tower block. He was clutching a beer bottle, and lurching unsteadily. The camera kept its distance as he paused to relieve himself against a garage door. Then they closed in on him. He smashed the bottle and lashed out with it, but they were quick and too many for him. Maybe they'd brought reinforcements this time. Soon he was lying in the shadow of his own urine, and the chant began.

But this time, it was different. They seemed to have a more definite agenda. Most of the kicks were to the head, and they continued after the victim had apparently lost consciousness. The sense of ritual was stronger than before. And the song repeated on one line, like a stuck record. *Je te batterai le face – Et le face, et le face – Et le face, et le face – Et le face, et le face...* Eventually they stopped. The boy was covered in blood and shattered glass. The twins lifted him by the arms and propped him up against the garage door. His head fell forward until it was almost touching the gravel.

The blonde girl stepped forward. The camera showed her face, coated with sweat. She was breathing hard. The chorus rose around her: *Alouette, je te batterai.* Her foot drew back, then lashed out in a steady, powerful arc. I didn't see it land, but I saw a dark object fly between two of the other youngsters, spattering their jeans with red. The camera moved back to show the gang standing around the twisted body. The picture was as still as a single frame.

When the screen blacked out, I threw the mobile away from me; it struck the wall with a dull thud. Sweat stung my eyes. I stumbled to the bathroom and knelt with my head over the toilet for several minutes, retching. Only a clear liquid, like developing fluid, came up. Slowly the images began to recede, still there but possible to disregard. I curled up on the vinyl floor of the bathroom and slept.

The next day at work, I wasn't quite as tired as I'd been for the last week. Regular mugs of black coffee enabled me to keep going. Late in the afternoon, I went into the kitchen to refuel and saw Alice, my manager, standing by the window. She was crying. Embarrassed, I muttered 'Sorry' and backed away. But she said, 'Ian, can I talk to you?'

'Sure,' I said, thinking she must have had a row with her boyfriend.

Alice bit her lip and turned back to the window, then said quietly: 'I've been getting phone calls in the night. Video messages. Know what I mean?' I said nothing. 'Last night they showed me my brother Mark getting beaten. And today he's not answering his phone. I'm scared to call the hospitals. I don't want to know what's happened. Mark's got a drug problem. He's been known to steal things. I don't talk about him much.'

She paused, staring at me. 'Have you had these messages too?'

There was nowhere else to look. 'Yes,' I said. 'I have.'

'Who do you think it is?'

I shrugged. 'Some gang, I don't know.'

She shook her head wearily. 'It's not that simple. You know how, the last few months, the papers have kept saying the government's finished unless it deals with the crime problem? I think this is their answer. It's not just a gang, Ian. It's a punishment squad.'

'Maybe you should go home,' I said. 'You're worried about your brother, that's understandable. But you'll probably find he's okay.'

Alice looked at me with something more like her usual managerial disdain. 'At least you're willing to admit you've seen them.' She walked past me and out of the kitchen. By the time I'd made myself a coffee, she was gone.

That night, the phone didn't ring. After a couple of hours, I got up and went out with the mobile in my jacket pocket. Apart from a few cars, the streets were deserted. No beggars, no drunks, no prostitutes. I could hear the voices chanting somewhere in the distance. *Alouette, gentil Alouette.* They were calling me. They didn't use the phone to call me, just to keep me in my place. When they wanted to call me, they sang.

As I walked up the long poorly-lit road through the industrial estate, I could hear the chant getting steadily louder. They weren't far away. I wondered what part of me their boots would strike first. When I got to the canal bridge, I stopped and switched off my phone.

The voices were getting louder as I raised the black Nokia to my face and smashed it hard against my mouth. Then again, striking my cheekbone, tearing the skin. And a third time, cracking a tooth and making me fall to my knees. Bile flooded my mouth, and I almost blacked out. But I kept on hitting myself in the face with the blood-soaked phone until the chorus began to fade.

Eventually, there was silence. I wiped the phone on my sleeve and stood up, leaning on the steel bridge. My face was stiff with bruises, and I could barely see. I walked slowly back towards the Swan Centre, thinking that I'd better take a day or two off sick while my face healed. I didn't think my manager would care too much. The memory of what she'd said to me was fading. I couldn't even remember clearly what she looked like, though I had a feeling I'd see her face again soon.

THE SLEEPERS

The coaches left from Digbeth at seven in the morning. It had snowed heavily the day before, and although the main roads were mostly clear the snow had frozen on side roads, pavements and car parks. Michael wasn't used to getting up this early on a Saturday; he felt like his head was still on the pillow, though his body was stepping carefully around patches of ice on the street.

More than a thousand people had gathered at the meeting place, where nine or ten coaches were waiting. Michael recognised a number of friends among the activists selling papers and the foot soldiers giving their names to the organiser. There were pensioners, schoolkids, mothers with babies. He hoped there wouldn't be any trouble; the previous weekend, he'd heard, a London demo had been attacked by a police squad.

This early, the roads around Birmingham were relatively quiet. Banks of snow glistened like flawed marble on the roadside surfaces. Weak sunlight filtered through the sky. Michael caught scraps of bitter conversation from the seats around him: *over a thousand civilians now... dropping white phosphorus on schools and hospitals... calling them 'human shields' for terrorists that aren't there* ... He was used to not quite believing things like that. But the times were testing his scepticism, and it was beginning to fail. That was why he was here.

As the coach's heating system kicked in, the chill softened. Michael felt his eyelids starting to close. He tried to focus on a cheaply printed newsletter about the invasion, with photos of grey faces emptied by death. The man in the next seat was determinedly sending text messages and ticking names off a list. Music was playing from the back of the coach. In the window, hedges and fields held up flowers of ice, non-life echoing life. Michael rested his face on his own shoulder and drifted into an uneasy sleep.

He was woken by the coach leader announcing that they were about to stop at the motorway service station, and would be moving on in fifteen minutes. Michael glanced out of the window and saw a hillside coated with snow. For a moment, he thought the curved white surface was made up of thousands of small faces: children with their eyes shut and their mouths just open, as if asleep. He rubbed his eyes. Bad news and an early morning start were getting to him.

Outside the service station, a fountain had frozen overnight. The ice was twisted into white sculptures. Hundreds of people were milling around the car park, their breath clouding in front of their faces. Michael bought a coffee and took it back to his seat. As they set off, the coach leader made a speech warning them to keep to the planned route and avoid confrontation with the police. He went on to rehearse the coach in a number of anti-war chants. Routines like this seemed faintly ridiculous when compared to the horror of reality. But it was easy to be paralysed by that. To say *What can you do* like it wasn't even a question.

After two hours of crawling through London, the coach reached Hyde Park Corner. Already, the park was covered with people. The coach group found the rest of the Birmingham contingent and waited while various people, some of them famous, spoke from a platform Michael couldn't see: there were too many banners and placards in between. A hundred thousand people, the organisers said. Ice crunched under their feet as they set off towards the exit. The sky was a blank page.

It was a long, slow march through streets lined with tall buildings that glittered with frost. Michael was holding a placard with imitation bullet holes going through it. In spite of the gloves, his hands were stiff with cold. Chants spread like echoes through the crowd. As they neared the end of the route, the police became more numerous until they were flanking the road on both sides, walking back and forth through the march. And then the road was blocked by police vans and a line of officers with riot shields. *Don't they realise that will cause the very thing they claim they're preventing?* Michael asked himself. Then realised it was a naïve question.

The cold was worse when you couldn't move. Someone threw a stink bomb from a window to land in the crowd. After half an hour, most of the demonstrators started to head back. They detoured through side-streets, then retraced the march's route, leaving placards scattered by the roadside. Michael stayed with a group of Birmingham people, including the coach leader – who took a call on his mobile phone and then told them there'd been a fight at the road block. A demonstrator had a broken arm. The police had knocked an elderly man to the ground and kicked him. A shop window had been broken.

The journey home was slow and rather subdued. Michael was on a different, less well-heated coach. As it crossed over the Thames, he looked down onto the frozen water. Once again, he could see countless faces trapped in the ice, repeated like crystals. Their eyes were closed. He looked up at the constellation of city lights in the stained night sky. Though physically tired, he didn't feel as sleepy as before. He got into a long conversation about socialism with the young woman sitting next to him, and tried not to look at the window.

When the coach returned to Digbeth, the city was veiled by mist. Michael caught the train home. He had only one uneasy moment, when the snow on the station roof revealed itself to be a patchwork of silent faces. When he got back to his flat, he lit the gas fire and poured himself a drink before turning the TV on. The news report said 'a few thousand' people had marched in London to protest against the war, and that property had been damaged. The new mayor of London was quoted as saying the demo had cost the city over a million pounds. There was a film clip of a shop window being smashed, broken glass spraying over the pavement.

The next day, the death toll in the occupied country had risen by two hundred. There was talk of a ceasefire protocol being drawn up by the United Nations. Meanwhile, across England the snow was still not melting. Michael saw the

THE SLEEPERS

faces everywhere, like a watermark: in front gardens, on the canal, even in frost-coated windows. But not in the pictures of snow that appeared in the papers or on TV. A few times, he saw people staring at the ice or snow in a confused way. He wondered if he might not be the only person who could see the sleepers.

The ceasefire protocol failed, both sides rejecting it. After several hundred more deaths, nearly all of them on one side, the invading country declared an end to its campaign. This had the effect of silencing all criticism of it in the press. The BBC refused to screen a disaster relief appeal on the grounds that the need for relief was a matter of political opinion. A medical journal that published an account of the casualties was deluged with complaints.

On Tuesday, in his lunch break, Michael was walking along Broad Street near the city centre. The canal was still frozen, putting a halt to the barge trips that catered for local evening parties. A sign warned people not to skate on the ice. Two young office workers, a man and a woman, were standing on the bridge. His arm was around her waist. She was pointing out over the canal. 'Look at the snow. Can you see? It looks like it's full of little faces... What's wrong with them?'

Temperatures were falling all over the country. On Wednesday, there was another heavy snowfall. Trains and buses were cancelled; Michael worked from home, emailing the files to an empty office. In late morning, he went out to buy some food. The faces were everywhere: on car roofs, in shop windows, even underfoot. Always the same narrow features, closed eyes, slightly open mouths. Their silence underlay every sound. He could see a few tiny hands reaching towards the light. Suddenly he thought of his past lovers, how much he'd liked watching them sleep.

How did he know the faces were asleep and not dead? He stood on a street corner, dazed, trying to answer that question. There was a tension in them, and their eyes were always shut. Could he see movement under the pale eyelids? What were they dreaming about? That question disturbed him so much he walked hastily to the cornershop and back home without looking at the snow. White flakes cut through the air and settled on his face and hands, melting to fine droplets.

That night, Michael sat up late, drinking cheap brandy. His sleep was thin, held together only by fear. Shadowy figures moved across his field of view. He couldn't see what they were running away from. Eventually he gave up, had a quick shower and got dressed, then went out. It was five in the morning. The road was empty but there were a few people in the distance, walking towards the city centre. He started walking after them, though he wasn't sure why. Maybe someone could explain the faces to him. He still felt half asleep, but it was the wrong half.

As he walked, Michael noticed how many people were standing in doorways or looking out through windows. The snow was frozen so hard that his feet barely left an impression on it. Whenever he looked down, the faces were there, packed together as if in a mass grave. He couldn't feel the cold anymore. The nearer he got to the city centre, the more people there were in the streets. Walking or standing, their eyes fixed on the snow.

The main square was nearly full of people. They were all staring up at the Town Hall roof, or down at the pool and fountain. More people were walking up from Broad Street and the Business Quarter. Nobody was speaking, or looking at anyone else. They were all watching the snow. Michael walked on past the library until he reached the stairs leading down to the expressway going north. From there, he could see that the car parks and grass verges, the canals and walkways, were all covered with a pale scar tissue of children's faces. They were clearer than ever before. More people were standing with him on the stairs, waiting for the dawn. For what would happen when the ice began to melt, and the children woke up. How their screams would tear the landscape apart.

ACKNOWLEDGEMENTS

Thanks are due to the editors of the publications in which these stories first appeared:

'The Brand', *Dark Dreams 2*, 1985.
'Tell the Difference', *Skeleton Crew 7*, 1991.
'Power Cut', *Skeleton Crew 10*, 1991.
'Empty Mouths', *Exuberance 4*, 1991.
'The City of Love' (as 'The Public Domain'), *Dementia 13 issue 12*, 1992; revised version in *Summer Chills* ed. Stephen Jones, Carroll & Graf, 2007.
'Every Form of Refuge', *Water Baby: Panurge 23* ed. John Murray, Panurge Publishing, 1995.
'The Last Cry', *Roadworks 12*, 2001.
'After the Flood', *The Darker Side* ed. John Pelan, Roc, 2002.
'The Hard Copy', *The 3rd Alternative 32*, 2002.
'All Beauty Sleeps', *Evermore* ed. James Robert Smith and Stephen Mark Rainey, Arkham House, 2006.

'Blue Train', *At Ease With the Dead* ed. Barbara and Christopher Roden, Ash-Tree Press, 2007.
'Alouette', *Subtle Edens* ed. Allen Ashley, Elastic Press, 2008.

Thanks are due to Steve Green for major technical support, and to Lesley Ward for letting me include her evocative artwork 'Roussalka'. Thanks also to Simon Bestwick, Dan T. Ghetu, John Howard, Ella Lane, Gary McMahon, Nicholas Royle, Chris Morgan, Mark Valentine, Julie Wilson and Tindal Street Fiction Group.

JOEL LANE

Joel Lane was the author of two novels, *From Blue to Black* and *The Blue Mask*; several short story collections, *The Earth Wire*, *The Lost District*, *The Terrible Changes*, *Do Not Pass Go*, *Where Furnaces Burn*, *The Anniversary of Never* and *Scar City*; a novella, *The Witnesses Are Gone*; and four volumes of poetry, *The Edge of the Screen*, *Trouble in the Heartland*, *The Autumn Myth* and *Instinct*. He edited three anthologies of short stories, *Birmingham Noir* (with Steve Bishop), *Beneath the Ground* and *Never Again* (with Allyson Bird). He won an Eric Gregory Award, two British Fantasy Awards and a World Fantasy Award. Born in Exeter in 1963, he lived most of his life in Birmingham, where he died in 2013.

Influx Press is an independent publisher based in London, committed to publishing innovative and challenging literature from across the UK and beyond.

www.influxpress.com
@Influxpress

THANKS TO OUR KICKSTARTER SUPPORTERS:

Tristam Adams
Daniel Appleby
Simon Avery
Jennifer Bernstein
Peter Burton
Ray Carne
Matthew Colbeck
Edward Cooke
Sam Cowan
Ant Firth-Clark
Bill Godber
Gareth Hopkins
Andy Howlett
Rob Jackson
Peter Keeley
Dominic Lyne
Andrew McAinsh
CM Muller
Matt Neil Hill
Jonathan Thornton
George Ttoouli
Goutham Veeramachaneni
Tom Wootton
Teresa Young